"Do you enjoy humiliating me?"

Sally's words were wooden as she went on. "If so, get your kicks now." Sally fought back tears. "I am indebted for the protection you've given Zambezi Safaris—and you're right, I would sell my soul to keep it going."

"And your body, Sally?" Paul asked with chilling venom. "Is that still part of the deal?" He clamped her wrist tightly as she tried to slap his face. "Don't you like to be reminded of your love for me?"

"Let go of me," she pleaded, avoiding the glittering coldness of his eyes.

"I will when you tell me one thing, Sally," he whispered softly as he slowly drew her to him. "Who do you love now?" he asked as his mouth sought hers.

Kate Proctor is a British writer who has lived most of her adult life abroad. Now divorced, she lives near London with her two grown-up daughters and her cat Wellington. She is a qualified French teacher, but at present devotes all of her time to writing.

Raindance

Kate Proctor

Harlequin Books

TORONTO • NEW YORK • LONDON
AMSTERDAM • PARIS • SYDNEY • HAMBURG
STOCKHOLM • ATHENS • TOKYO • MILAN

Original hardcover edition published in 1988
by Mills & Boon Limited

ISBN 0-373-17026-2

Harlequin Romance first edition November 1988

CHAPTER ONE

THERE were times when the English climate seemed hell-bent on living up to every derogatory remark ever passed on it, and this particular October day was one of them, mused Sally Hughes idly as the steady beat of rain quickened its tempo against the windows. Not that this day was any worse than the past five or six, she reminded herself, glancing up from her desk as the outer door of the office flew open to usher in a blast of rain-chilled air along with the trench-coated figure of a man.

Relief at the prospect of distraction from twiddling her thumbs and listening to the rain brought a smile of welcome to Sally's attractive features.

'Zambezi Safaris?' There was no answering smile from her unexpected visitor, just that abrupt enquiry and the impatient toss of his head that sent droplets of rain flying from the gleaming black of his hair.

Sally nodded and immediately began praying that her eyes were not out on stalks as he stepped further into the light and began shedding his raincoat. It was quite some time since her gaze had fallen in such spontaneous interest on a man, she realised with a wry pang, but this particular specimen was quite something. He was tall, perhaps an inch or two over six feet, she gauged, and the impeccable and patently expensive cut of his clothing displayed his athletic body to perfection—broad-shouldered, yet lean and slim-hipped.

By now quite engrossed in her inspection, she decided she had slight reservations about the eyes—blue flecked with steel that somehow conveyed an innate coldness despite the dark, silky profusion of surrounding lashes. But it was the face itself that claimed her undivided attention. Though almost routinely handsome in the classical mould of its features, the overall impression was anything but one of mere routine good looks...the mouth took care of that.

'I'd like to speak to Miss Hughes.'

Sally was still preoccupied by that mouth as she acknowledged her name. There was unmistakable strength in the boldness of its lines, but there was also a fullness, especially about the lower lip, that was quite aggressively sensual—in fact, it was that disconcerting blend of coldness and sensuality that rendered that face so strikingly attractive.

'The name's Morrant—Paul Morrant,' he informed her, the cold eyes narrowing now in barely concealed impatience.

Sally's leisurely assessment of his looks came to a jolting halt as her mental alarm system went into overdrive. 'Come to rant at me in person, have you?' she demanded through clenched teeth.

'If necessary,' he informed her brusquely.

'Well, it won't be necessary—we have nothing more to discuss,' she snapped, then made a concerted effort to tone the anger from her voice. It was pointless letting this conversation deteriorate into the slanging matches they had exchanged over the telephone. 'There's nothing more I *can* say. I've explained this company's position to you time and again.'

'Obviously not to my satisfaction,' he observed tersely, slinging the damp raincoat over one dark-suited shoulder and sauntering towards her desk. 'For a company such as Zambezi Safaris to lose a client is bad enough.' There was an hypnotic softness in the beautifully modulated voice. 'But, having managed to do so, to show such total lack of concern is somewhat less than satisfactory, wouldn't you agree?' He dropped his coat across the back of one of the chairs before her desk. 'It sounds more like downright negligence to me.'

The scathing sarcasm in his tone affected her now as it had on every previous occasion, though this time there would not be the luxury of escape by slamming the phone down on him.

Clinging to the shreds of her rapidly disappearing control, Sally rose. 'Mr Morrant, I don't propose indulging in yet another slanging match with you,' she informed him with all the patience she could muster. 'I can only repeat that we did not "lose" Jonathan Wincombe, as you insist on putting it. He arrived in Zambia according to schedule and then opted out of the entire safari programme.'

'And that's that as far as you are concerned?' he demanded icily.

'What more do you expect?' she exclaimed impatiently. 'We can't actually force clients to participate in the safaris they've booked, despite what you seem to think to the contrary, Mr Morrant.'

'So—he's not the first,' he countered quickly. 'Tell me, Miss Hughes—these clients of yours who pay such considerable sums for your company's tours and then mysteriously opt out of them—how many have failed to leave Zambia on the scheduled flight out?' As he spoke, he lowered himself, uninvited, on to one of the chairs, his shrewdly impersonal gaze never once straying from the slim figure before him.

Relieved to have him no longer towering over her, Sally also sat down, her hands unconsciously reaching up to

sweep away from her face the mass of tawny blond hair
that fell to her shoulders. The eyes on her noted the
gesture, just as they had noted an almost imperceptible
shadow darken her open features. But where other male
eyes tended to register frank appreciation of such deli-
cately boned loveliness, the eyes of Paul Morrant were
no more than coolly assessing.

'Our clients aren't in the habit of dropping out in
droves.' She sounded defensive, she realised warily, but
his remarks had triggered off doubts lurking unexam-
ined at the back of her mind. Now was not the time to
be examining them, she warned herself with a stab of
alarm as they leapt to the fore.

The season now mercifully drawing to a close had
hardly been the most satisfying in her life—there had
been too many doubts and uncertainties. In many ways,
she had needed her seven-month period of virtual iso-
lation in the leafy lushness of Guildford—a world away
from Africa. The day-to-day running of the office,
Zambezi Safaris' sole European centre, had been
routine—boring, if she were honest—but finalising the
company's accounts for the previous year, while keeping
a close eye on the current year's figures, had proved an
increasingly depressing exercise. No wonder other
problems had been relegated to the back of her mind,
she told herself gloomily; problems such as the fact that
Jonathan Wincombe had been by no means the first of
their clients to arrive in Lusaka and announce his with-
drawal from the scheduled programme. Oddly enough,
her scowling, unwelcome visitor was right; as far as she
knew, Jonathan Wincombe had been the only one not
to take the return flight from Lusaka. Though appalled
by such casual throwing away of what amounted to
thousands of pounds, Sally had found it relatively easy

to push Jonathan Wincombe and the others to the back of her mind—whether earned or not, Zambezi Safaris had at least received payment in full from them. What she had not found possible to ignore had been the handful of long-standing clients who had dropped without warning from the booking lists—those had undoubtedly cost the company dearly.

Paul Morrant's remarks about other cancellations had certainly hit a vulnerable spot, but they could only have been a shot in the dark, she consoled herself, and unconsciously squared her slim shoulders as she met once more the hostile impatience of his gaze.

'Mr Wincombe did mention to my partner there was a likelihood he'd be making his own departure arrangements.' She struggled to mask her growing annoyance as she saw his expression harden. 'Yet another point I've already made to you on the phone.' Probably just before the last time she had slammed it down on him, she fumed inwardly. His autocratic and abusive manner on the phone was bad enough, but infinitely preferable to his arrogantly overbearing presence.

'I've no idea how you run your business, Miss Hughes. Perhaps it would not be a matter of concern to you if one of your employees were to take three weeks' leave and fail to show up after five.' The voice was ominously soft, a softness negated by the action of tanned, elegantly tapering fingers drumming their impatience against the arm of the chair. 'I don't happen to hold that view and, though I have far better things to do with my time than chase around Africa looking for Wincombe, it looks as though I have no alternative.'

Everything about him, from the tone of his voice to the slightly menacing aura of power that seemed to exude from every pore of his impeccably clad body, set Sally's teeth on edge. In her line of business she came across more than her fair share of men such as Paul Morrant— wealthy, autocratic and used only to snapping their fingers to get what they wanted. Though she fervently wished it were not the case, it was only within the means of the very wealthy to savour the majesty of African wildlife at close quarters. But she had yet to come across one as blatantly arrogant as this particular man—let alone one who could bring her to gibbering fury by merely opening his supercilious mouth!

More to prove to herself that she was still capable of exercising control than from any wish to mollify him, she injected a modicum of civility into her voice as she reiterated what she had already told him several times before.

Silently, she was cursing not only him but also the truant Jonathan Wincombe—a man she had never found particularly appealing. For several years a regular client of Zambezi Safaris, he had not been typical of the many Europeans who fell instantly in love with the dark continent, though that had been his claim the few times Sally had met him. She found it surprising to learn that he actually held down a job, probably because she had mentally classed him in the role of feckless playboy. His superficiality had grated on her, just as had his assumption that all women would find his boyish good looks irresistible. Perhaps many would, but Sally had been obliged to let him know in the plainest of terms that she was not one of them.

'I'm afraid that's all I can tell you,' she finished, the glimmer of hope that she would soon be rid of him allowing her to sound almost conciliatory. 'Mr Wincombe is plainly at fault for not advising you of his whereabouts, but we can hardly be held responsible for that.

For you to go haring off to Zambia to look for him would be a complete waste of your time. Why don't you...' She was silenced by his exclamation of anger as he rose to his feet.

'When I get to Lusaka,' he stated coldly, 'I intend seeing this partner of yours. And I hope to God he proves more competent than...'

'He happens to be a *she*, and the competence of neither of us is in question,' retorted Sally, fury darkening her eyes to navy as she leapt to her feet and glowered across the desk at him. 'Anyone would think Wincombe was a wayward child instead of a grown man! Just who the hell do you think you are, to...'

'If you don't know who I am, Miss Hughes, perhaps it would pay you to find out.' There was open threat in his silkily uttered words. 'And then, when I tell you the end of this particular season could well be the end of Zambezi Safaris, you will know that I'm not a man to indulge in idle threats.' His left brow, a perfectly formed wing of black, was arched in contempt, but it was the glitter of something more disturbing than contempt in the chill blue of those eyes that stifled the disbelieving laughter rising to Sally's lips. The man was obviously unbalanced.

'You must be out of your mind,' she whispered, determined to ignore an irrational unease that was seeping through her. 'Completely out of your mind.'

Yet he looked so utterly sane as he moved unhurriedly towards the door—sane and totally self-assured as, with a shrug of indifference, he drew his coat across the expanse of his shoulders.

'And, if you insist on going,' called out Sally defiantly, 'good luck with my partner—she'll be even less intimidated by your bullying tactics than I am.' Even as she uttered them, she was cringing at the childish tone of goading in her words.

'Is that so?' he asked softly, turning and smiling as he reached the door—except that smile was hardly the term for that sudden flash of even white teeth against the deep tan of his skin; not when accompanied by the deadpan chill that emanated from the eyes above. 'Perhaps your partner has less to hide than you.' Before she could challenge that infuriatingly enigmatic statement, he continued, 'Should you decide to co-operate, though, Miss Hughes, do ring me. But re-member, in a very few days I shall be forced to take the matter into my own hands.'

'Just what the hell did he mean—Lena might have less to hide than I do? The man has the knack of reducing me to gibbering rage in a few seconds flat!' wailed Sally, then gave a groan of contrition.

She had resolved to keep the matter to herself when she visited Eddie Kapotwe in hospital that evening. But Eddie knew her too well, she thought guiltily. He had sensed the anger still simmering in her and had drawn it all out within minutes of her arrival.

'Oh, Eddie, I shouldn't be burdening you with all this,' she exclaimed unhappily.

The Zambian let out a groaning protest of a laugh. 'Sally, I've spent over two years flat on my back, both here and at home, while that crazy wife of mine and her equally crazy partner have bent over backwards to shield me from the facts of life.' He chuckled. 'Don't you think it's time you and Lena removed those completely un-necessary kid gloves? Soon I'll be a hundred per cent fit, and back with my conservation team within a few months...but where will Zambezi Safaris be then, Sally?'

Sally refused to meet his eyes, unsure of what he might be getting at but certain that Lena wanted him protected from their present troubles—Eddie had had enough troubles of his own.

'You might as well face it, love, it's a lot worse than a few last-minute cancellations and losing some of your regulars.'

Sally tried to keep her face expressionless, puzzled that he knew as much as he did but positively alarmed by his statement that there was more.

'You'll be losing two guides and half a dozen aides at the end of this season—now, in fact. I dare say Lena will be breaking the news to you when you get back.'

'Who told you this, Eddie?' croaked Sally. 'Certainly not Lena.'

He shook his head, smiling gently at her. 'We conservation lads have a very soft spot for Zambezi Safaris. My team have had their eyes and ears open ever since I've been laid up—they've always kept me informed.' He patted her hand in an attempt to dispel her obvious consternation. 'Sally, it was their duty. Zambezi Safaris means too much to all of us . . . it's what got Jonas and your father started, and it's part of what will help us turn the dream of those two great men into reality.'

The softly spoken words filled Sally with equal proportions of pride and pain. It was almost fourteen years ago, she thought sadly, that her father, Peter Hughes, and Jonas Mwenya, Lena's father, had met at a London seminar: where the English zoologist and the Zambian botanist had discovered a common dream—to protect and preserve Africa's natural heritage for the generations yet to come.

Within three months, and accompanied by his ten-year-old daughter, Peter Hughes had returned to Zambia,

the country in which he had spent much of his own
childhood. Within three years, thanks to the single-
minded determination of both men, Zambezi Safaris was
a thriving and lucrative business, providing the bulk of
funds to support their most pressing aim—the eradi-
cation of game poaching in areas hitherto unprotected.
With the Government of Zambia one of their staunchest
allies, they had organised networks of dedicated and
highly qualified conservationists throughout East and
Central Africa, linking up with already established
groups. Although they had achieved much in the ensuing years, there were still areas where greed prevailed
and where those in power did little to curb the very lucrative slaughter of game.

It was on a fact-finding mission to one such area that
Peter Hughes, Jonas Mwenya and two of their aides had
been brutally murdered by poachers just over two years
previously. And it was there that Eddie Kapotwe, orig-
inally a botanist like his newly acquired father-in-law
before him, had been left for dead—his back crushed
by the impact of the fleeing poachers' vehicle. Over a
year later, and with three bouts of major surgery behind
him, Eddie had been flown to the famous Surrey hospital in which he now lay, where another team of experts
had begun the painstaking task of bringing mobility back
to his traumatised spine.

Married scarcely six months before the tragedy that
had devastated so many lives, Lena Kapotwe had stayed
in England by her stricken husband's side. She had returned to Zambia only after receiving the news for which
they had all so fervently prayed—that, given time, there
would be no trace of the paralysis once feared permanent.

Sally made a concentrated effort to drag her mind away
from the pain of the past. No matter how bad things

might seem, there was always the miracle of Eddie's recovery to replenish their hopes. With a barely perceptible squaring of her shoulders, she smiled tentatively at him.

'Lena and I have weathered far worse than this,' she stated.

'Of course you have, love,' encouraged Eddie, puzzled by the uncertainty in her tone. 'Sally, am I right in thinking this guy really managed to get under your skin this afternoon? It's not like you to sound so down.'

Sally sighed. 'You're one hundred per cent right,' she admitted with a rueful grin. 'I'm stupid to over-react like that, but men like Paul Morrant...'

'Hold it!' interrupted Eddie frowning. 'What on earth has Paul Morrant to do with this?'

'He's the one giving me all the hassle,' exclaimed Sally impatiently, then hesitated on seeing his obvious concern. Suddenly her mind was filled with the echo of those softly menacing words: 'If you don't know who I am... perhaps it would pay you to find out'... 'Eddie, who is this man, for God's sake—the Mafia?'

His soft chuckle did little to lessen her increasing apprehension as she tensely awaited his reply.

'There's nothing in the least shady about Morrant, I can assure you,' murmured Eddie, his tone preoccupied. 'Though I've a feeling tangling with the Mafia would give you slightly better odds than crossing him, should he choose to throw his weight around.'

'But I've never heard of the man,' protested Sally.

'How about Morrant-Gervaise-Morrant?'

'The merchant bankers?'

Eddie nodded. 'Except this guy *is* Morrant-Gervaise-Morrant... owns it lock, stock and barrel,' he mused.

'Which makes him just about one of the most powerful men in Europe in terms of wealth.'

'How come you know so much about him?' asked Sally, her apprehension deepening. 'Merchant banking's a bit far removed from your line of work, Eddie.'

'You're wrong, Sally,' he sighed. 'Men like Morrant are crucial to my line of work—especially when they support the conservation programme to the tune of millions as he does.'

The man she had been ranting at like a fishwife, thought Sally, cursing her luck, then quickly reminding herself he had asked for all he had got.

But the reminder brought her little comfort and, as Eddie took her step by relentless step once more through that afternoon's encounter, she was gripped by a sense of foreboding that refused to budge despite all her attempts to dismiss it as irrational.

'I know it's unusual for an employee to take an extended holiday without informing his employer,' she admitted reluctantly. 'But you have to look at it in perspective, Eddie. Paul Morrant's such an overbearing bully—Wincombe probably knew the only way he'd get extra leave was by simply taking it.'

'Sally!' Eddie's tone was sharp. 'Conjecture is pointless. You'll have to contact him and try to get to the bottom of this. You have no option,' he added gently as she flashed him a look of shocked disbelief. 'He was **right when he said he doesn't indulge in idle threats**— men that powerful don't have to. And if he wanted to fold up Zambezi Safaris you'll have to face the fact that he could.' He raised a silencing hand as she began to protest. 'It's up to you to find out why he should even consider doing so.'

Suddenly Sally's senses returned to her. 'Eddie, this is daft,' she stated firmly. 'As the company's accountant, I can vouch for it's financial integrity, and Lena's one of the best international lawyers around where it comes to a business like ours. Between us, there's no way anyone could wind Zambezi Safaris up—not on any grounds.' This time it was she who raised the silencing hand. 'I promise it isn't a case of my just digging in my heels because I find the wretched man so objectionable. Eddie, when he snapped his fingers I couldn't have jumped even had I wanted to—I've no idea where Jonathan Wincombe is. He could have left Zambia on the next flight out for all we know.'

'That could be checked,' observed Eddie, tugging pensively at his lower lip. 'You leave for Lusaka the day after tomorrow, right?'

Sally nodded.

'And Lena's due here a couple of days after that.'

Again she nodded, unsure of what he was getting at.

'So...should Morrant decide to descend on Lusaka, the person lumbered with him would be you, love,' he finished with an apologetic grin.

Sally pulled a small face and sighed—she had not bothered to think that far ahead; as far as she had been concerned there was no point in doing so. But Eddie's troubled expression indicated otherwise.

'Sally, there's obviously more to this than meets the eye...and besides, by seeing him before you leave you **could well be saving yourself further hassle in the long** run.'

There were a million things Sally could think of more appealing than the undoubted humiliation of going cap in hand to the likes of Paul Morrant. But Eddie Kapotwe was a man whose opinion she valued above most...and

the expression on Eddie's face was a disturbing reflection of the inexplicable unease that clung so tenaciously in her mind. And besides, if any threat, however
remote, hung over Zambezi Safaris, her pride would automatically take a back seat

'OK, *Bwana*,' she announced with a doleful grin. 'The
lamb will prepare itself for the slaughter.'

CHAPTER TWO

ODDLY enough, Paul Morrant had not gloated when she had rung him the following morning—a point Sally kept reminding herself of each time her spirits took a dive. If anything, he had sounded somewhat preoccupied when he had agreed to meet her the next day at the West End offices of Morrant-Gervaise-Morrant.

Perhaps the hounding of poor old Wincombe had been replaced by another whim, she speculated hopefully as she boarded the Tube from Heathrow. The thought lifted her flagging spirits a fraction—the sooner she had this meeting behind her, the sooner she could dismiss the obnoxious Paul Morrant from her mind and relax before catching her evening flight to Lusaka.

Tomorrow she would be back in the sunshine with a vengeance, she told herself wryly as she stepped from Piccadilly Underground and into the familiar, dismal drizzle. She was still finding it impossible to conjure up the oppressive heat that always preceded Zambia's November rains when she reached the imposing façade of Morrant-Gervaise-Morrant's London headquarters.

She made her way through heavy plate-glass doors and into an atmosphere of discreet, though unmistakable, opulence. There was no such thing as 'discreet opulence', she informed herself, disgruntled, as she gave her name to one of two immaculately groomed and almost flawlessly beautiful receptionists. By the time she had reached the director's suite on the fifth floor she had roughly deduced that the cost of furnishings alone could

probably have financed one of Jonas and her father's
field groups for the best part of a couple of years. This
uncharitable train of thought was further encouraged by
the vision of perfection who asked her to take a seat—
almost a clone of the other two, thought Sally in mild
disbelief, and had a sudden mental picture of Paul
Morrant imperiously selecting his female staff from
contingents of Miss World finalists.

It was only when Eddie's remark about the merchant
banker's contributions to the conservation programme
crept unbidden into her mind that her vitriolic train of
thought ceased.

But any charitable feelings the memory may have
stirred had long since dispersed when, over half an hour
later, there was still no sign of the man she was to see.

'My appointment was for midday,' she testily informed the girl at the desk, glowering furiously as she
did so.

'I feel dreadful about this,' apologised the girl, with
a friendly smile of sympathy. 'That meeting should have
finished ages ago. Unfortunately, it's one I daren't
interrupt.'

No, thought Sally in complete understanding, the ogre
she worked for would no doubt have had her publicly
lynched for such a liberty. But she was filled with remorse for her small-minded ungraciousness.

'I'll hang on for a while longer,' she murmured, an
unspoken apology in the warmth of her smile—had it
not been for the girl she would have upped and left now.

'Would you like me to rustle you up a coffee?'

Before the girl had finished speaking, the heavily pan-
elled door at the far end of the room opened and two
men emerged. Seconds later, jacketless and with his shirt
sleeves rolled up to reveal strong, deeply tanned arms,

Paul Morrant appeared at the doorway and proceeded to stretch like a huge, luxuriating cat.

'Oh, God, it's you!' he exclaimed, pausing mid-stretch as Sally leapt in fury to her feet.

'How gracious of you to notice,' she snarled as he strolled towards her.

'I really am sorry,' he apologised, taking the wind out of her sails with the unexpectedness of it, then frowned down at a wafer-thin gold watch nestling against the dark hairs of his wrist. 'That was a nine-thirty appointment that turned into a three-hour battle. Gina, why the hell didn't you buzz me?' he demanded of the girl at the desk.

'It's hardly her fault,' butted in Sally sharply before the girl could reply, and was promptly thrown by what could only be described as a rueful grin.

'I'll take full blame, Miss Hughes, and let Gina off her stint in the dungeons if you agree to our talking over lunch—I'm starved.'

Nonplussed, but with her blood still dangerously close to boiling point, Sally nodded—it seemed she had little option.

Her face was still tight with suspicion as he led her into the softly lit warmth of a nearby restaurant.

'You'll put me off my food if you're going to sit and glower like that,' he remarked blandly as they were handed menus.

'No doubt *you* are all sweetness and light when you've been kept waiting the best part of an hour,' she retorted, her eyes glued resolutely to the menu.

'It was thirty-six minutes...OK, OK.' He held up a placating hand as her eyes hurled daggers across the table at him. 'I owe you a string of apologies. I've had a lot on my mind recently and I'm afraid you were subjected

to the backlash of it.' As apologies went, it was hardly
fulsome, and Sally lost no time telling him so.

'If there's a certain verbal format you require for an
apology, just jot it down and I'll recite it to you,' he
retorted, his face adopting its familiar scowl.

'You'd probably choke to death on such unfamiliar
words,' responded Sally acidly, then her eyes flew suspiciously to his—the man had actually chuckled.

Perhaps something on the menu had amused him, she
thought savagely, and proceeded to give the waiter her
order. But she found herself surreptitiously scrutinising
him when he followed suit. He really was quite disgust-
ingly attractive, she thought with a slightly bemused detachment, and found the term 'face of an angel' springing
incongruously to mind. A bad-tempered, macho and decidedly sensuous-looking angel, she decided, the ghost
of a disbelieving smile creeping to her lips as she observed the sweeping fan of silky black lashes shadowed
against his cheek and wondered if he ever resorted to
batting them to get his own way.

'Do you plan on sharing the joke?' he demanded, de-
tecting that fleeting smile.

'I was under the impression we were here to discuss
Jonathan Wincombe's whereabouts, not to exchange
jokes,' she responded frigidly, annoyed with herself for
her straying thoughts. Beautiful he might be, but he was
still the man whose scathing sarcasm had reduced her
to gibbering fury in the past.

'So, you know where he is, do you?' he asked, fixing
her with that disconcertingly cold gaze of his.

'No, I don't!' she exclaimed angrily.

'Why did you ask to see me, then?'

'Because when someone storms into my office and
threatens to close down my business, it seems politic to

co-operate—especially when it turns out they have the clout you allegedly have.'

'A wise decision—though you took your time arriving at it,' he remarked with a lack of tact that infuriated her.

'I'm sure it will come as no surprise to you that the decision had little to do with me,' she informed him through clenched teeth. 'Quite frankly, if it were up to me, I'd tell you to take a running jump, Mr Morrant, because there is no legal way you or anyone else can touch Zambezi Safaris.'

In the short respite that came with the arrival of the hors-d'oeuvre, Sally grappled with her rapidly dwindling temper, uncertain whether it would be wiser to leave now or stay in the hope she could last the meal out without actually flinging part of it at him.

'As usual, this is in danger of deteriorating into a brawl,' he stated as the waiters departed. 'So why not accept my apology and then we can take it from there?'

His apology? Sally had difficulty in believing her ears. She placed a forkful of food into her mouth, chewing slowly as she counted to ten—then she swallowed the mouthful along with her pride.

'Done,' she managed when her mouth was completely empty and found herself on the receiving end of a quite stunning smile. With a smile like that to switch on at will, there would never be any need for him to resort to batting his eyelashes, she reasoned truculently, and glowered at him.

'So—now that we're bosom buddies,' he murmured, choosing to ignore her look, 'I'll try to explain my predicament. You see, that fool Wincombe has put Morrant-Gervaise-Morrant in rather a spot. Normally, an extended holiday on his part wouldn't be crucial—the man's not exactly renowned for his reliability—but this time it's vital that we contact him as quickly as possible.'

'If it's that urgent, and he's still actually in Zambia, we could arrange for police messages to be broadcast,' offered Sally.

'Good God, no! That's the last thing I want,' he exclaimed. 'You're obviously not too well acquainted with the world of international banking,' he continued with a soft chuckle. 'It's not quite the done thing to send out police messages for missing personnel, even if it is only to say Aunt Flo's broken a leg.'

'And has his Aunt Flo suffered such a fate, Mr Morrant?' asked Sally, her expression softened by amusement.

'I'm quite sure, if he possesses such an aunt, that she's still intact . . . and the name is Paul.' There was humour in his voice and a hint of laughter had crept into his eyes, both of which Sally noted with a wary detachment. It would take a darn sight more than the odd flash of charm to lull her into believing this was the true Paul Morrant she was now seeing—though charm, she was beginning to suspect, he possessed in abundance when the mood took him.

'Do you know anything about computers, Sally?'

'I use a small one for Zambezi Safaris, though I imagine it's nothing as complex as a company your size would require,' she told him, wondering where this could be leading.

'Complex being something of an understatement,' he remarked pensively. 'A couple of months ago our two top computer men were involved in a motorway pile-up...our number one, a close friend, didn't survive. His deputy is still in pretty bad shape, but at least he's going to make it.'

Where charm had failed, the expression she now saw on his face went a long way to lessening her residual hostility. No stranger to grief herself, Sally had no doubt that the death of his friend and the injuries to the survivor had affected him deeply.

'The reason I'm telling you this is that Wincombe was given acting control, and with it our top security access codes.'

'He hasn't done anything illegal, has he?' asked Sally and immediately found herself the object of a cool, oddly enigmatic, gaze.

'Whatever makes you ask that?'

She shrugged. 'I don't know...secret code numbers...high finance.' And a vivid imagination, she thought, feeling slightly foolish.

'Well, don't let your imagination run riot,' he advised, almost as though he had read her thoughts, and amusement softened the harsh line of his mouth. 'The truth of the matter is that our Geneva branch needs access to certain data—though why this particular set should even be on a security rating is beyond me, but it is—and Wincombe's irresponsibility has left us in the embarrassing position of not being able to produce it from our own bloody computer!'

His disgruntled expression made it plain how little used he was to being subjected to inconvenience, and it brought a chuckle that was almost sympathetic from Sally.

'Oh, dear! You'd have saved yourself quite a bit of time had you told me this at the start,' she told him, then added with forthright candour, 'not to mention both of us a lot of unpleasantness.'

The waiters arrived with their main courses as she spoke and he made no reply but, for the briefest of moments, his eyes widened in what she suspected was displeasure—and then he began to laugh. It was low and rumbling and altogether pleasing to the ear, and it also danced its way into his eyes.

'I suppose I asked for that,' he murmured once the waiters had left.

'There's no suppose about it,' she informed him primly, then smiled despite herself.

She was rewarded by another stunning, though completely contritionless, smile before he turned his attention to his food.

'Are you certain it's irresponsibility on Jonathan Wincombe's part?' she asked, voicing a worrying doubt. 'He could be ill...or something,' she added lamely as she was subjected to a look of exaggerated patience.

'If you knew Wincombe, you'd know it was far more likely to be the ''or something'', and the odds are it would come in female form.'

'Having met him on a couple of occasions, I can understand your train of thought,' she murmured wryly.

'Oh, dear, I'm sure you would,' he observed with that chuckle she was beginning to find so infectious.

'Our first priority is to find out if he's still in Zambia,' she informed him briskly, resisting both his laughter and the gentle teasing now in his eyes. 'Our airline contacts should be able to trace if and when he left. Then, if he's still there, it shouldn't be too difficult to have him located.'

She went on to tell him of her imminent departure.

'So, had I hotfooted it over there, it wouldn't just have been the formidable partner I'd have to contend with,' he mocked gently.

'Lena's not in the least formidable,' she protested, quickly dismissing the ridiculous suspicion that Paul

Morrant might be indulging in a spot of exceedingly subtle flirtation. 'Not that you'd have had the opportunity to find out for yourself,' she added, and from there found herself explaining the treatment Eddie was undergoing and the terrible events that had led up to his needing it.

'All in all, the pair of you have had a grim couple of years of it.' His tone was shocked. 'His injuries must be a constant reminder to both of you of what happened to your fathers.'

Sally looked at him in surprise. As time had passed, so few people had been able to understand precisely that—the terrible memories evoked day in and day out by the sight of that once so active body stilled almost to the point of death.

'I found it tough, but it was a living nightmare for poor Lena. But this time when she returns home, it will be with Eddie by her side, as fit as he ever was...and then the memories will have a chance to fade in all three of us.'

Abruptly she changed the subject, outlining her plans for finding Jonathan Wincombe, should the eventuality arise, and during those hesitant moments it took for the immediate pain of remembering to subside she was grateful for the understanding within Paul that allowed her to ramble uninterrupted.

'Very thorough indeed,' he commented when she had finished. 'Though there is one thing. Apart from not wanting MGM's name bandied about...' he broke off as a waiter arrived and ordered coffee when Sally declined a dessert '...it's imperative that Wincombe doesn't know he's being sought. Let me explain,' he added hastily as she flashed him a look of sheer incredulity. 'I can't afford to have him panicked. You see, given time, he'd

no doubt eventually turn up with a load of leaky excuses
circumstances would oblige us to accept. But time we
don't have, and I've a feeling he could well drop everything and bolt if he hears I'm after him. He's not the
type to handle a head-on confrontation, and responsibility is a word that doesn't appear to feature in his particular vocabulary.'

'But if he ran he'd stand no chance whatsoever of
keeping his job,' protested Sally.

Her words were met with an eloquent shrug. 'With a
fairly comfortable private income such as Wincombe
possesses, losing his job would create no hardship...it
just increases the likelihood of his taking the easiest way
out.'

'So what do I do if I run across him?' enquired Sally.
'Hitch him to the nearest baobab tree and await your
further instructions?'

'Sounds a mite strenuous,' he murmured and again
gave that lazy rumbling chuckle. 'Do you run to telex
in your Lusaka office?'

Sally grinned as she nodded. 'We found the drums so
unreliable.'

'I've a feeling poor Wincombe discovered he'd bitten
off far more than he could chew the day he came up
against you, Sally Hughes.' This time there could be no
doubting it: the teasing tone, but most of all the hint of
challenge in those disturbing blue eyes, told her he was
definitely flirting.

What surprised her most of all, though, was her un-
deniable inclination to respond. While part of her immediately smothered that inclination, another openly
rejoiced.

In the days before her heart, and probably to a greater
extent her pride, had taken such a metaphorical bat-

tering at the hands of Mark Shelby, a similar response
to a man such as Paul Morrant would have brought her
no surprise—she was a perfectly normal woman, and
even at his scowling, abusive worst there could be no
denying that, physically, this was an exceptionally attractive man. But her experience with Mark had seemed
to have put an end to all that, she thought with a twinge
of bitterness that was surprisingly pain-free. And now,
unexpected and ill-judged though her present reaction
to Paul Morrant might be, it was a response none the
less, and it was her first concrete evidence that time was
indeed a healer, and that Mark and all the heartache he
had brought her were beginning to take a back seat in
her memory.

'The link between that and telex eludes me,' she replied lightly, while an inner voice warned that, though
her pleasure was understandable, flirting with this particular man could well turn out to be as harmless as attempting to house-train cobras.

'There is none. But you'll need my personal telex
number, and also my private telephone number, should
you need to contact me out of office hours.'

He took a card from his wallet, jotted down both and
handed it to her 'What time is your flight to Lusaka?'
He frowned at her reply. 'Good God! You don't have
to trail all the way back to Guildford for your things,
do you?'

'I'm a little better organised than that,' protested Sally
with a laugh. 'I dropped my luggage off at Heathrow
on the way here.'

'If you'd told me about your flight when you rang, I
might have been able to arrange a better time for you,'
he murmured apologetically. 'Now you're left with an
afternoon to kill.'

'But I'm looking forward to it,' protested Sally. 'There's an exhibition on at the Royal Academy I've been meaning to see—and now I can.'

Paul pulled a wry face. 'I'd love to join you, but I'm afraid that's impossible.' He glanced at his watch. 'In fact, we've only time for another coffee before it's back to the grindstone for me.'

He blinked in amazement as Sally burst out laughing.

'It's just as well,' she chuckled. 'Somehow I can't imagine you trailing round an art gallery in order to assuage a misplaced feeling of guilt. Had I felt the time you suggested inconvenient, I'd have asked for another.'

'And in no uncertain terms, too,' he murmured, his amusement obvious. 'But I assure you, guilt has little to do with my wishing I could accompany you...Modigliani happens to be one of my favourite painters...it is the Modigliani exhibition you want to see?'

Sally nodded, amazed that he should know of the exhibition. She watched as he ordered more coffee and found herself puzzling over her amazement. She knew nothing of this man and his tastes, she reminded herself, and had, therefore, no grounds on which to feel such surprise.

'So, you're a Modigliani fan,' he observed, as the waiter left.

'I can't honestly say that I am,' she confessed a little shyly. 'My father was, and he always regretted having taken me to a Modigliani exhibition when I was far too young to appreciate it. He used to joke that he'd try again when I was mentally mature enough...but we never got round to it.'

He glanced at his watch again as the waiter returned to refill their cups. 'I'd have liked the chance to recap

on what you'll do, should Wincombe still be in Zambia.'
He grinned at her suddenly. 'And I'd be very interested
to hear how you get on with Modigliani.'

Sally watched in perplexed amusement as he drained
his cup.

'I'll meet you outside the Academy at six—that way
I'll be able to kill two birds with one stone.'

At the dot of six o'clock, Sally entered the foyer and
spotted Paul Morrant by the doorway, the glossy
darkness of his head bent towards the brochure in which
he was engrossed.

'Well, what's the verdict?' he asked, glancing up as
she reached his side.

Sally hesitated, still lost in the melancholy beauty of
the world she had just left. 'I'm not sure if I could put
it into words,' she sighed, enraptured. 'But I understand
what my father meant . . . why he was so captivated . . .'
She gave a small shrug of embarrassment as words
seemed to desert her.

'Am I to take it you've joined the ranks of the well
and truly hooked?' he asked with a soft, throaty laugh.

'Oh, yes,' she breathed contentedly. 'Though heaven
knows how I'm going to come sufficiently down to earth
to discuss anything as mundane as tracking down
Jonathan Wincombe,' she added with a rueful smile, as
they stepped out into the unrelenting drizzle.

'Your return to earth is inevitable, but drowning isn't.'
He watched in amusement as she unconsciously shook
off the rain beginning to cling to her hair. 'We'd best
make a dash for my car,' he told her, taking her lightly
by the arm as they joined the residual swell of the rush-
hour crowds. 'We can go over the Wincombe business
on the way to the airport.'

'You don't have to take me to the airport,' she protested, running to keep up with him as he lengthened his stride. 'I can easily take the Underground.'

'And I can just as easily drive you.'

She didn't argue; less because it would have been a waste of breath to do so than because she had very little inclination. When he eventually helped her into a large, gleaming white BMW, she leaned back against the luxury of red leather upholstery and gave a small grin of pleasure.

'The Tube wouldn't have been a patch on this,' she murmured as he intercepted the grin and raised questioning eyebrows.

But the Tube would have been a darn sight more restful, she was later telling herself in groaning resentment as, for the umpteenth time, he took her through the plans they had discussed earlier. Her reaction to his favourite painter had had nothing to do with his meeting her again, she fumed silently; he simply hadn't finished grilling her!

And it was almost as though he doubted her mental competence, she thought with growing resentment as that soft, impersonal voice once again went over each minute detail.

He must be hell to work for, she told herself irritably, what with his foul temper and this ghastly, nit-picking perfectionism he was now displaying.

Though there were other sides to him, she reminded **herself with a twinge of guilt. There was the unex**pectedly sensitive man, who had understood immediately the terrible memories constantly evoked by Eddie's wounds. There was the man of culture who could delight in paintings, much as her father had. Then, of course, there was the man who had charmed her despite

herself—reawakening in her the ability to respond to the
subtle flattery of flirtation. All in all, she decided, the
odds seemed stacked in his favour and, though he would
never know it, she had much to be grateful for from this
decidedly complex and really quite fascinating man.

'What a shame we'll not be able to go over it a fifth—
or would it be a sixth?—time,' she murmured impishly
as they approached terminal three; her irritation now
completely gone. 'You can drop me off here.'

Ignoring her words completely, he made straight for
the car park. 'But if I see you off we could recap another
few times,' he informed her angelically, sliding the
powerful car to a halt. 'Sally, I realise I might have over-
done it somewhat—but it *is* important.'

'I know. But I've an aversion to being talked at as
though I were mentally defective,' she replied, her smile
taking any sting out of her words. 'And there's absolutely no need for you to come in. It was very good of
you to go to the trouble of driving me here.'

'I don't know about the mental deficiency,' he interrupted in deadpan tones. 'But the argumentativeness I
can definitely vouch for.'

With an amused shrug of defeat, she followed him
out of the car and found herself marvelling that he should
ever resort to anger to get his own way when he could
charm so effortlessly.

As they collected her luggage and had it weighed in,
Sally was discovering how difficult it was not to be
acutely aware of his presence—a point brought home by
the fact that just about every female between the ages
of sixteen and sixty openly treated him to a second, and
often third, look.

Yet he seemed almost oblivious of his effect on
women, she noted as the two girls at the check-in desk

vied for his attention—unlike Mark, she remembered
idly, who had always been calculatingly conscious of his
appeal.

Sally watched in fascination as one of the girls eventually addressed him and was subjected to the cool im-
placability of his gaze.

'I didn't catch what you said,' he informed the girl
politely.

'I asked if she was going off and leaving you all on
your own,' laughed the clerk, indicating Sally's ticket.

For a moment he frowned in puzzlement, then his face
lightened and he turned to Sally and gave her an
altogether heart-stopping smile. 'Perhaps, if you ask
nicely, you'd be able to take me on as hand luggage.'

Sally's attempt at a withering look had little success;
she had attempted it too soon after being subjected to
that smile. Paul Morrant might appear oblivious of his
effect on women, she thought in amused exasperation,
but at this particular moment she had a shrewd suspicion he was completely aware of the effect he was
having on her.

'Do you need magazines...a book?' he asked, while
his eyes mocked gently.

'I have a book in my bag,' she replied, unable to drop
her eyes from his gaze.

'Well, come along then, Sally Hughes, it's time we
bundled you off.'

He took her hand, his fingers lightly entwining in hers
and, as he led her towards the departure point, her mind
made its way back to that morning.

She had woken to a feeling that could only be described as dread, her mind recoiling from the unpleasant
prospect of once again facing one of the most objectionable men it had ever been her misfortune to meet.

And now here she was, hand in hand with that same man, and the thought that the journey, towards which he led her, would whisk her several thousand miles from him brought her a quite definite tinge of regret. With these thoughts in her mind, she looked up at him as they reached the barriers and gave a small, disbelieving shake of her head.

'I was remembering how much I dreaded meeting you today,' she told him in answer to the quizzical rise of his brows.

Something flitted across his face, so quickly that it was gone before she could interpret it, leaving only the inscrutable gaze of those heavy-lidded, half-opened eyes that hovered on hers. Then he drew her away from the waiting officials and into the seclusion of a nearby telephone cove.

'That was then...this is now,' he whispered softly, drawing her into his arms.

His lips, when they met hers, sent a shock of excitement through her with the breathless delicacy of their touch. Then there was the sweet moistness of his tongue on her mouth, parting her lips to claim and explore. The idea of resistance never occurred to her; instead, her arms crept up round his neck to allow her fingers their freedom to caress their way into the springy, night-black thickness of his hair.

What should have been a carefree embrace—the gentle meeting of lips in acknowledgement of the light-hearted mutual attraction that had heightened their few shared hours—swiftly deviated from its intended course almost from the moment of its inception. Mouths that should have been strangers clung in almost familiar welcome, as though rediscovering long-forgotten delights. Never a kiss of farewell, it became an inflammatory incitement

to passion that swept through Sally, possessing her in its
madness till she could only cling in complete oblivion
of her surroundings, in complete oblivion of all but the
arms and the lips that had caught her in their spell.

There was a moment when his arms tightened in
bruising fierceness, then suddenly she was free and his
hands were reaching up to cup her face, drawing her
away as though disembodied from the mouth that had
demanded and received such urgent response from hers.
There was gentleness in those hands as they brought her
to rest against the sharp rise and fall of his chest and,
as she struggled to impose a bearable rhythm on the
ragged disorder of her breathing, those hands hovered
on her shoulders, their weightless impersonality belied
by the heavy thud of his heart against her cheek.

In the moments of eternity it took to return from
madness to reality, Sally was filled with the terrible panic
of wondering how on earth she should react.

Then he spoke. 'I suppose there's no time left to go
over those plans just once more?'

The humour was undermined only slightly by the
husky breathlessness of his voice, but it had given the
lead Sally so needed.

She drew away from the sanctuary of his chest and
looked up at him, seeing the soft languor of passion drift
from his eyes to be replaced by the teasing gleam of
laughter.

'Still convinced you're dealing with a half-wit, I see,'
she murmured, her words a breathless, throaty whisper,
while silently she was thanking him for having returned
her so painlessly to earth.

CHAPTER THREE

'When did you pass your driving test, Alphonse?' croaked Sally, her eyes tightly closed and her hand aching from its fierce grip on the seat edge.

'Two weeks ago,' announced the gardener-cum-handyman with proud relish as he hurled the car around another corner and yet again clipped the kerb.

'Alphonse was all for letting you know the good news,' murmured Lena Kapotwe sweetly. 'But I convinced him it would be a lovely surprise if he picked you up from the airport.' She gave a yelp of protest as Sally's elbow dealt her a vicious blow to the ribs.

'How thoughtful of you,' muttered Sally, opening her eyes only long enough to glower threateningly at the grinning girl beside her. 'And what has Aggie to say about this driving?'

Alphonse Phiri roared with glee. 'She's worse than you, little Sally! You close your eyes, but Aggie won't even get in the car.' Startled by the apparent proximity of his laughter, Sally's eyes flew open to find herself face to face with the chortling chauffeur.

'For God's sake, Alphonse!' she shrieked. 'You're supposed to keep your eyes on the road!'

'Relax, we've made it,' murmured Lena, not even flinching as Alphonse lurched the car into the drive and missed one of the wrought-iron gates by a whisker. 'Aggie's doing her fatted-calf routine, so for heaven's sake tell her you're on a diet before she bakes us out of house and home.'

Limp with relief, Sally staggered from the car to feast
her eyes on the sprawling, creeper-clad house that had
been their shared home since she was ten.

She stepped inside the familiar, welcoming coolness,
savouring once more the rich russet gleam of tiled floors
and the stark simplicity of whitewashed brick walls. Then
she made her way to the vast galley kitchen and straight
into the smothering, tearful embrace of Aggie.

'I was terrified that fool husband of mine would have
you killed before he got you home,' fretted the
housekeeper.

'I'm still in one piece, love,' chuckled Sally, giving the
plump, motherly figure a tight hug. 'Aggie, I could smell
your baking a couple of miles down the road,' she
breathed contentedly. 'I can't wait to get my teeth into
one of your cherry buns.'

Her hand was smartly slapped aside as it reached
towards the tempting array on the kitchen table.

'Not till you've had your breakfast,' scolded Aggie,
reverting to her old self now she was satisfied her chick
was safe and sound. 'Off you go and get into something
cool; this heat will kill you after Europe.' Aggie's concept
of Europe was of a continent buried six feet beneath a
permanent blanket of snow, and she stubbornly rejected
any evidence to the contrary. 'You and Lena can eat on
the veranda, before it gets too hot to be out.'

Minutes later, dressed in a cool, flowing caftan, Sally
stepped out on to the veranda and spotted Lena at the
edge of the swimming pool, her long brown legs dangling
in the water.

'Think yourself lucky I didn't sneak up and heave you
in,' she announced, hitching up the flowing gown and
joining her grinning partner. 'No examiner in his right
mind could have given Alphonse a licence.'

'He's ghastly, isn't he?' chuckled Lena, then she sighed, her face growing serious. 'Sally, do you feel up to launching straight into business? It's something I feel we should get over and done with.'

Sally nodded, disturbed by the anxiety on her friend's face. 'We could have one of those high-powered working breakfasts,' she joked, as Aggie trundled a laden trolly on to the veranda. Lena gave a wan smile as she nodded and got to her feet.

'Lena, I know about the staffing problems,' offered Sally, rising also and following her. 'Eddie told me.'

'I know,' murmured Lena, the worry on her face being replaced by a look that was almost bashful. 'I had a terrible fit of the lonelies the other night and rang him. He told me all about your chat. Heavens, there's enough to feed a small army here,' she gasped as she began dishing out eggs and bacon. Her eyes widened suddenly. 'I forgot to ask!' she exclaimed. 'Was it an absolute ordeal yesterday with that ogre?'

Sally looked at her blankly.

'Paul Morrant,' prompted Lena impatiently. 'Eddie was convinced blood would be shed.'

'Well, it wasn't,' replied Sally, conscious of the colour that had rushed to her cheeks. 'He was under a lot of pressure the first time we met, but he's actually rather...nice,' she finished lamely.

'Nice!' snorted Lena indignantly. 'Nice people don't go around threatening to close down other people's businesses!'

'I'm sure he had no real intention of doing that,' protested Sally, ignoring the disquieting realisation that she had never got round to discussing that threat with him. She quickly explained the facts.

'I still don't see why he threatened to close us down, nor what he'd gain by doing so—apart from revenge, and it's hardly our fault that a fool like Jonathan Wincombe's gone missing.'

'Stop worrying, Lena. Paul's temper probably runs on a short fuse, but...'

'It's Paul now, is it?' interrupted Lena, her brown eyes suddenly gleaming with interest. 'And just how "nice" did he turn out to be?' she teased as the colour again rose in Sally's cheeks. 'Come on, Sally, spit it out!'

Sally gave a groan of protest, then smiled in exasperation at her grinning friend. 'God, you can be worse than Aggie at times...OK!' she squeaked as Lena threatened her with a bread roll. 'Physically, he's the most stunning specimen on two legs. Temperamentally, he ranges from positively foul to angelic. And yes, he did play havoc with the Hughes pulse-rate a couple of times during the course of the afternoon and that, Lena Kapotwe, is absolutely all there is to tell!'

'God bless you, Paul Morrant,' breathed Lena reverentially, raising her glass of orange juice in a toast.

Sally regarded her with amused exasperation. 'Lena, there's no need to get carried away, I can assure you,' she scolded. 'Heavens, if you saw him, you'd be worried out of your mind if I hadn't felt a bit of response.'

'And precisely how many men have you responded to since Mark?' demanded Lena, her voice utterly serious.

'Only Paul,' admitted Sally. 'But at least it's a start...and you can't imagine how relieved I am,' she added bashfully.

'And *you* can't imagine how relieved *I* am,' responded Lena forcefully. 'Sally, there have been so many things I've felt unable to discuss with you because they mean bringing up Mark's name... I've been dreading this talk with you.'

'I'm so sorry, Lena, you've had more than your fair share of worries as it is. But my problems over Mark is no longer one of them—I promise you. Is he one of the guides who's left?'

Lena nodded. 'And Josh Banda.'

Sally gasped. 'Two of our best.'

'Josh, yes,' agreed Lena. 'But Mark...he's been nothing but a liability since the first day of the season. He pulled out of over fifty per cent of his tours, often with practically no notice—and on health grounds, would you believe?'

Sally frowned in puzzlement. 'What's wrong with him?'

'Damn all,' snorted Lena. 'He's got himself a tame doctor who provides all the necessary paperwork. Your ex-fiancé has had more suspected ailments, none of which have come to anything, than half the population of Zambia lumped together.'

'But why, for heaven's sake?' Sally was finding it difficult to believe her ears—Mark had a lazy streak in him, but this was completely unlike him.

'Because he's set up his own operation. Quite obviously he hadn't managed to get a full season lined up— hence his deigning to turn up and carry out his duties to us now and then.'

'Lena, you should have let me know...you shouldn't have had to carry this worry on your own,' fretted Sally guiltily.

'Sally, for all I knew you still could have thought you loved the guy,' sighed Lena. 'How could I risk dragging up all your hurt for what could well have been only suspicions?'

'But they're no longer just suspicions, are they, Lena?'

The Zambian girl gave an unhappy shrug. 'The handful of our clients who stepped off the planes and out of our tours all happened to do so when our golden boy was allegedly ill. Three of them, including your missing Wincombe, were seen in his company. I've a feeling the majority of our missing regulars could also be down to him, though I doubt if I could prove it,' she finished grimly.

'To set up in direct competition to us...and in so underhand a way...' Sally fell silent, sickened by the thought.

'We might have lost a few clients to him.' Lena rose to her feet. 'But direct competition it isn't. There's something I have to show you.'

She returned moments later and handed Sally a single sheet of paper. 'I came across this only a couple of days ago.' At first Sally thought she was looking at a sheet of their own headed paper; the layout and lettering were identical. The difference, when she spotted it, sent her heart plummeting to her stomach.

Her eyes were dark with confused disbelief as they flew to Lena's and then once more to the paper. Where their stationery bore the legend 'Zambezi Safaris' this read 'Zambezi Trophies'. To Sally and to everyone concerned with conservation, the word 'trophy' in certain contexts was a mere euphemism for a slaughtered animal.

The sad irony of the conservation of wildlife was that, with success, there often came the necessity of herd-cropping to maintain the delicate balance so vital in the controlled game areas. And so, in successful and enlightened countries such as Zambia, the numbers and species of animals available to be hunted were governed by figures assessed by wildlife experts. Because hunting was such a lucrative business, the licensed hunting companies had never been known to exceed the permitted number of kills—the fines stipulated for such an act were crippling—and they tended to work hand in hand with the conservationists to eradicate illegal poaching.

Technically, the hunting companies fulfilled an inescapable need, Sally reminded herself, but theirs was a business her father and Jonas had detested. Though accepting the necessity of herd-cropping, both had regarded it as an unpleasant task to be carried out within the conservation programme, and not something to be turned into sport for the benefit of the bloodthirsty wealthy. Jonas had always maintained that hunting was like a drug to some who, once hooked, would think nothing of stepping outside the law to maintain that habit.

Sally gave a sigh as she handed back the paper. 'It's a legally registered company,' she stated quietly. 'And just because we hold our fathers' views on hunting, we can't simply impose them on Mark.'

Lena hunched her shoulders angrily. 'That company was registered in Mark's name almost a year ago...when he was still under contract to us.' She gave an angry exclamation at the puzzlement on her partner's face. 'For an entire season a senior guide in the employ of Zambezi Safaris has been organising and participating in hunting safaris...apart from the fact that it's against the charter of this company, and therefore against the law...and apart from the fact that one glance at this wretched paper would lead most into assuming this was a subsidiary of ours...' She broke off, rubbing her hands distractedly across her face. 'Sally, have you any idea what it could do if some bright spark got hold of this—put two and two together and got five? Not just to us, but to the entire conservation programme?'

The sight of Lena, whom little could ruffle, on the verge of tears only confirmed the sick fear filling Sally.

Suddenly she understood only too well. To the well-meaning, but often unenlightened public, killing was killing no matter what reasons there might be for it. One whiff of scandal, however remotely linked to the conservation programme, and their sources of income, running to millions annually, could be lost overnight. From the big multi-nationals supplying transport and equipment, down to the small textile firm that provided the Tanzanian network with its bush clothing—all were in it for the prestige advertising it engendered and all would respond instantly to what would undoubtedly be negative public reaction to the idea of a company founded to finance the protection of wildlife being linked, however unwittingly, with its slaughter.

'Lena, what in God's name can we do?' she whispered hoarsely.

'What can we do—except keep our fingers crossed?' muttered Lena, her face tense with frustration and anger. 'I keep telling myself that Mark can't possibly be aware of the potential damage to us from his actions. I've no idea where he is at the moment, but you'll have to find him and speak to him, Sally.' She reached out to pour the coffee, her hand shaking. 'For a start, all that headed paper will have to be found and destroyed. Try to talk him into changing the name of his outfit . . . he can call it anything he likes as long as by no stretch of anyone's imagination could it be linked with us. God, how could he be so bloody thoughtless?' she finished despairingly.

'Lena, I'll do everything I can,' vowed Sally, any misgivings she might have felt about a confrontation with

Mark buried beneath her shock. 'I want you flying off to Eddie without business worries on your mind.'

Lena gave her a wan smile. 'That's a pretty tall order...we've not even compared accounts yet,' she sighed. 'And Lusaka's don't look all that healthy to my untrained eye.'

They began discussing figures in earnest, talking in terms which, to an outsider, would imply an exceedingly healthy margin of profit, even if it were somewhat down on previous years. But Zambezi Safaris was no ordinary company; it existed solely to provide the shortfall between the Zambian Government's contribution to the country's conservation network and the actual costs.

'Let's face it, Sally, we're not going to make it.' Lena's voice was despondent. 'You and I have been drawing subsistence salaries as it is, and there's no chance of getting more out of the Government—the price of copper's at rock bottom.'

The Zambian economy relied heavily on the income from its huge copper mining industry and had suffered badly from years of slumping copper prices. Both girls were acutely aware of how fortunate the conservation programme was to still get Government backing.

'I'm sure things will look better when I've had a proper look at the books.'

'Well, don't go into a frenzy of excitement when you see the latest bank statement,' warned Lena with a small chuckle. 'Our Alice in Wonderland bank have been up to their old tricks—a few days ago one of their kindly clerks credited our account with a couple of million *kwacha*.'

Sally's eyes widened in amused disbelief—in sterling, that was about one million pounds.

'For a while they almost had me believing our fairy godmother had pitched in,' grinned Lena. 'Naturally they whipped it off us, eventually—though only after a couple of days battling to convince them on my part.' She laughed. 'You know, they're so incompetent, yet you can't help but admire the way they sail on in blissful oblivion of the fact.'

'They're an accountant's nightmare,' groaned Sally, but there was affection in her protest. At times they had been driven to tearing their hair out by the frequent incompetence of their Lusaka bank, but in their heart of hearts they knew they could never move their business elsewhere—it had been the only financial organisation prepared to stake Peter and Jonas when they had started out.

'I'll go through the bank statements with my usual fine-tooth comb,' promised Sally. 'But there's plenty of time for that. I'd best contact the airlines about Jonathan Wincombe and get him out of the way first.'

'Of course, you realise we might as well wind up the company now if he went on one of Mark's hunting expeditions,' exploded Lena with a sudden bitterness. 'And everything points to his having done so.'

'Lena, stop being so defeatist,' begged Sally. 'It's not like you. I'll explain to Paul...'

'Are you out of your mind?' gasped Lena. 'Sally, he's the *last* person you can mention any of this to. Morrant-Gervaise-Morrant finance the entire Ugandan network, according to Eddie.'

'Lena, he'd understand,' insisted Sally. 'He's...'

'He's a very successful businessman,' interrupted Lena. 'And no matter what you might think, I'm telling you! He'd cut his company's links before you had the last words out of your mouth. Then the avalanche would start.' She grasped both Sally's hands in hers, her expression pleading. 'Sally, for all I know this guy could fancy you like mad, but it wouldn't alter the fact that, when it comes to business, all he'll be considering is the gut reaction of the public and its effect on Morrant-Gervaise-Morrant! Sally,' she begged. 'Whatever happens, promise me you'll never tell him anything of this—it would finish Zambezi Safaris—not to mention...'

'All right, I promise,' agreed Sally unhappily. 'Anyway, Jonathan Wincombe might never have been involved with Mark,' she added, injecting an optimism she did not feel into her voice.

'He was seen with Mark only a couple of weeks ago,' Lena informed her gloomily. 'But I suppose we can only clutch at straws. Sally...' She hesitated, then continued, 'Are you really over that creep?'

Sally smiled across the table at the girl then topped up their cups.

'I am,' she announced positively. 'You see, that's why what happened yesterday means so much to me...it had little or nothing to do with Paul Morrant as a person. It was just that an attractive man decided to flirt a little and I responded. It was as though something had switched off inside me after Mark...and now it's been switched back on...am I making any sense?' she asked hesitantly.

Lena nodded. 'It was like a wall—there were so many things I wanted to say to you but couldn't because of it.' She paused, reaching out to stroke back the tawny blond hair from Sally's face in a gesture that was almost maternal. 'While part of me grieved for the pain you endured, the rest of me rejoiced that at last you'd seen him for what he was. You know, I was almost at my wits' end when the two of you set a wedding date.'

It had been with less than three months to go till their wedding that Sally had let herself into Mark's flat early one morning. Knowing he would begin a two-week safari later that day, she had resolved to pin her disorganised fiancé down to numbers—the way he had been inviting all and sundry, it would be out of the question to hold the reception at her home.

'Come along, lazybones, decision time,' she had called out as she marched into his bedroom.

Those had been the last words she had ever spoken to him: she had turned and marched straight out again, Mark's softly groaned oaths ringing in her ears alongside the protesting tones of the redhead sharing his bed.

Though the memory was fresh in every detail, the searing pain was no longer there—nothing but a futile twinge of regret for what might have been had Mark Shelby ever been the man she so foolishly had believed him to be.

'My poor Lena,' she whispered. 'What on earth were you going to do?'

'God knows,' sighed Lena. 'But Tony Fernandez and Kasempa Ndhlovu had given me an ultimatum the day before you found out—tell you before the week was out, or they would.'

So Tony and Kasempa—and probably all the other company guides—had known, thought Sally with a small stab of wounded pride, but she was inordinately relieved to discover just how small it was.

'The strange thing is, I've a feeling Mark actually believed he loved you,' mused Lena. 'As far as he's capable of loving anyone other than himself. The trouble is, he thought he could have his cake and eat it. You have to admit, you were the only one he was prepared to marry.'

'The reason for that probably being that I'm the only woman he's ever shown interest in who has refused to jump into his bed,' chuckled Sally.

Lena burst out laughing. 'So I was right, you were never really in love with him anyway.'

'Of course I was,' protested Sally indignantly. 'It's just that I didn't feel obliged to leap into his bed to prove it.'

'Hmm,' grunted Lena, grinning infuriatingly as she shook her head.

'Hmm all you like, partner dear, but I have to get cracking with the airlines,' muttered Sally, feeling it wiser to drop the subject.

Jonathan Wincombe's name had not appeared on any departure list to date. But, as Sally had pointed out to an increasingly gloomy Lena at the airport that morning, last-minute bookings were often not recorded on flight lists.

'If you do find him, you'll have to appeal to his better nature, if he has one,' Lena had stated, obviously resigned to the fact he was still in the country. 'Just as long as Paul Morrant doesn't get wind of any of this...who knows, with an endless string of luck we might even claw our way through.'

Sally attempted to get her mind sorted out as she made her way straight from the airport to the office. It upset her to think Lena had so much on her mind—the fact that she would soon be returning with a completely fit Eddie should have been her only thought.

Still feeling unsettled, she let herself into the office and tackled her first task—telexing Paul Morrant to inform him that, as far as she could ascertain, Jonathan Wincombe could still be in Zambia. Her mind refused to settle down to its second task—that of going through Lena's meticulously kept books.

Damn Mark and his thoughtless, selfish stupidity! Damn Jonathan Wincombe for pretty much the same thing, and damn Morrant-Gervaise-Morrant for their paranoid penchant for secret codes!

No wonder she found it impossible to concentrate, she told herself despondently. Subterfuge in any form was anathema to her, and here she was embroiled to her eyeballs in it. She had promised to put Paul Morrant in touch with Wincombe—a promise she would now be unable to fulfil until she had spoken to the missing man herself. She found herself wincing at the memory of Paul's unfounded insinuation that she had something to hide—her indignation had been total—and now, after his having confided in her, there was terrible irony in the fact that she had *everything* to hide.

'I understand what you mean about a Zambian October—it's like a bloody inferno.'

Sally started noticeably; in fact, she almost leapt out of her skin at the familiar sound of that softly drawling voice.

'What on earth are you doing here?' she croaked, her vocal cords seizing up on her as he moved in soundless tread towards her, his handsome face curiously expressionless.

'You look as though you'd been caught raiding the petty-cash tin,' he observed softly, still no discernible expression on his face.

'I . . . I've just sent you a telex,' she managed, struggling to find a shred of composure.

'No doubt to tell me Wincombe's still here,' he stated, flinging his tall athlete's body into a wicker chair and proceeding to fan himself vigorously with a sheaf of papers lifted from her correspondence tray. 'Don't you run to air-conditioning around here?' he complained, managing to look the epitome of cool composure to Sally, who felt her cheeks were guilt-stained scarlet.

'I'll turn on the ceiling fan,' she offered, leaping to her feet and knocking over the waste-paper basket in her haste to reach the switch and escape the shrewd cool gaze of those eyes. 'The rains will be here any day now, they usually come on the fifth—it will be much better then,' she gabbled, standing with her back to him and giving an inordinate amount of attention to the simple task of depressing the switch.

'Remember, remember, the fifth of November,' he chanted, further unnerving Sally with the oddly toneless edge to his voice.

'You still haven't told me why you're here,' managed Sally as the ponderous swoosh of the overhead blades started up.

'I had word that Wincombe was definitely here,' he informed her, shrugging his way out of his pale, tropical-weight jacket as she returned to her desk.

Sally's eyes widened momentarily as he appeared to be about to do the same with his shirt.

'Sally, you have to understand that time is a vital commodity where I'm concerned.'

'A point you've already made,' she observed sharply. 'But it happens to take time to get the information you require; such as the fact that the airlines have no record of his having left,' she added, her hackles beginning to rise. Careful, she warned herself as he made no reply, and she watched as he applied his attention to his shirt sleeves, rolling each above the elbow to display arms dark with tan and a silky covering of hair.

'Would you like a cup of tea?'

It was the cool, mocking gaze beneath the eyebrows raised in mild disbelief that told Sally her words had sounded every bit as ludicrous to his ears as they had to her own.

'There's beer in the fridge over there,' she snapped and sat down. God knew why she hadn't stuck to her original opinion of him, she thought angrily as her eyes met that cold blue gaze of his. Charm was obviously a commodity he used only to suit his ends—and it was plain he no longer felt the need of it now.

Her eyes dropped to the firm, unyielding line of his mouth, and the sudden memory of the effect those lips had wrought on her sent a shiver of unwelcome excitement coursing through her. Desperately she made an attempt to pull herself together.

'Perhaps you should tell me what you've heard—then we can see about finding Mr Wincombe as quickly as possible.' Under the circumstances, she could only feel pleased that her voice sounded almost normal. The panic into which his unexpected arrival had thrown her served as a stern warning. Whatever happened, she would need to keep a complete grip on herself—and a very close watch on Paul Morrant.

'Perhaps you'd care to go over those plans once again.' The voice was utterly matter-of-fact, but the eyes that met hers contained teasing laughter, and the relief that flooded through Sally seemed to knock the breath out of her.

'I think the best thing we can do is get you to your hotel,' she smiled and was surprised to find relief could make her sound so happy. 'I take it you've come straight from the airport. Where are you staying?'

'Actually, I've just come from the hotel at which I was under the impression I was staying,' he revealed, going over to the fridge and helping himself to a beer. 'The positive booking my secretary made yesterday doesn't seem to hold good today. And they inform me all the other hotels are full.'

'Of course—there's a trade fair on in Lusaka,' remembered Sally. 'The hotels are notorious for overbooking when that happens.' She was racking her brains to think who she could ask to put him up, discarding name after name that sprang to mind. All of them knew Mark and all could quite innocently say far too much should Paul Morrant decide to start asking questions.

'It looks as though I'll be playing hostess—you'll not find anywhere else.' And that way she would be able to keep the closest of watches on him, she comforted herself, while attempting to dismiss the realisation that he would be able to keep a similarly close watch on her.

'I take it we'll be suitably chaperoned?' he murmured as he raised the can to his lips once more. 'I'd hate your reputation to be jeopardised because of your kindness.'

'Don't give it a thought. Aggie, our housekeeper, would guard my honour with her life,' she laughed, amazing herself with her hitherto unsuspected capacity for lying. Aggie would happily hand her over to the first man who showed a modicum of interest—her view being that any woman approaching twenty-four and still unmarried was distinctly disadvantaged!

CHAPTER FOUR

'THAT *Bwana* Paul looks good enough to eat—though I suppose you've already noticed.'

'No, I haven't!' muttered Sally, her eyes darting anxiously to the doorway. 'And for God's sake stop saying things like that, Aggie, he'll hear you,' she pleaded.

She must have been out of her mind bringing him here, she told herself frustratedly. Aggie had practically set to work on a trousseau the moment she had clapped eyes on him, and it was an altogether nerve-racking experience just having him underfoot. She had been reduced to a jittery bag of nerves when Eddie had rung unexpectedly—quaking lest Paul emerge from the pool, where he had taken up residence for the best part of the day, and overhear the conversation.

At least Eddie had derived satisfaction from the banker's accommodation problems.

'You'll be able to stick to him like a leech and make sure nobody inadvertently spills the beans.'

And precisely how was she expected to contact Mark, she wondered morosely, while constantly in Paul Morrant's sights? One thing she was learning—and learning with a vengeance—she was definitely not cut out for this cloak and dagger routine. She would be a nervous wreck in next to no time.

'Aggie! There'll be enough potato salad to feed an army by the time we've made up this lot,' she complained.

54

'A man built like that needs his food,' observed Aggie appreciatively, her eyes beaming their approval as they alighted on the dripping form strolling through the doorway.

'That's what I like to see,' grinned Paul Morrant, trailing wet footprints in his wake. 'Two women slaving to their hearts' content for my benefit.'

'Hearts' content, my ass,' growled Sally, glowering pointedly at the pool gathering on the floor as it dripped its way down the glistening, magnificently proportioned body. 'I do believe you could teach Alphonse a thing or two when it comes to male chauvinist piggery.' She winced as Aggie's roar of laughter blasted her eardrum.

'He certainly could,' chuckled the woman, leaving no doubt that her words were complimentary.

'When are you coming for a swim, Sally?' he demanded, reducing her to shrieking protest as he shook his dripping hair over her.

'When I've finished this,' she muttered, dragging her attention back to the salad.

Paul Morrant, she had quickly discovered, was hyperactive. On arrival, he had had a marathon session on the phone and, judging by the resultant stream of calls ensuing thereafter, had passed her number to just about every business contact he had.

When not dripping all over the phone, he had spent his time ploughing up and down the pool in a powerful, effortless crawl—obviously a man with limitless energy to burn.

Sally glanced at her watch and frowned. It was almost six and, as always in this part of the tropics, it would be dark soon—and she was dying for a cooling dip in the pool.

She was just about to suggest he took a turn at potato chopping while she got into her swimming things, when the phone rang.

'No doubt that's for you,' she observed resignedly, and found herself unconsciously inspecting the broad, muscled expanse of his departing back.

There was no denying he had the body of a Greek god, she mused idly. And, given his disconcerting predilection for swanning around practically naked, as he had for the best part of the day, she had had ample opportunity to view its perfection.

'If you haven't noticed that one, there's something wrong with your eyes, girl,' smirked Aggie, missing nothing.

'Aggie, it takes more than just a beautiful body to get me interested,' sniffed Sally dismissively.

'Oh, yes? That's all Mark Shelby ever had,' chuckled Aggie. 'And he hadn't much up here,' she added, tapping her head. 'This one's got it all up here and what's more, the body's bigger and better.'

'Aggie!' groaned Sally pleadingly as Paul padded in again.

'That was my secretary, at long last,' he announced. 'Wincombe's staying in Kabwe, in a place called Jacaranda Pools—ever heard of it?'

'Hang on a second, will you, Paul?' Sally gave him an apologetic grin, grabbing Aggie by the arm as she opened her mouth to speak. 'I'm about to flake out—I'll join you in the pool.' Her fingers dug warningly into the housekeeper's plump arm. 'And Aggie, if you don't produce those bikinis of mine from where you've hidden them, on the double, I'm going to chuck you in the pool.' Shoving the protesting woman ahead of her, she made her way to her room.

'Your bikinis are where they always are,' objected an outraged Aggie, as Sally closed the door behind them.

'I know they are, love,' placated Sally. 'Please . . . just listen. We have a very big problem.'

She quickly slipped into a black bikini as she explained, and heaved a huge sigh of relief on discovering that Lena had already told Aggie of Mark's treachery.

'But you have to understand that Paul is a very important man . . . and very powerful. Aggie, if he learns *any* of this, Zambezi Safaris is finished—he'll close us down.'

Aggie sat on the bed, her kindly face troubled. 'He wouldn't do something like that, not if you told him the truth,' she declared stubbornly. 'Only lies would make a man like him angry enough to do that.'

'Please, Aggie,' begged Sally. 'I have no choice! I can't tell him—I've promised Lena I won't.'

There was no time to try to explain the intricacies of prestige advertising to Aggie—it was probably a complexity of European culture she would find impossible to comprehend, Sally realised with a stab of envy.

'I'll say nothing—you know that,' promised the housekeeper. 'But how are you going to lie your way out of the fact the man he's looking for is staying at the Shelby place in Kabwe?'

'I've no idea,' sighed Sally. 'But I'll have to come up with something.'

'I'd better get Alphonse to put on the pool lights,' muttered Aggie, getting to her feet. 'It'll be dark soon.'

One look at Sally's uncertain face as she examined her reflection in the full-length mirror quickly restored Aggie's ebullient spirits.

'*Bwana* Paul's really going to appreciate that,' she observed, with a decidedly dirty chuckle.

'Aggie, I'm sure I've something less revealing than this,' fretted Sally, rummaging frantically through a drawer.

'No, you haven't, and it's never troubled you before—so why should it now?' remarked Aggie with infuriating complacency. 'You've a good pair of *majumbas* on you—perhaps a bit on the small side,' she added, observing her own massive bosom with pride. 'And a lovely pair of legs a real man would...'

'Aggie! Shut up, will you?' shrieked Sally, grabbing a towelling robe.

With Aggie's raucous cackles still ringing in her ears, she fled to the garden and dived straight into the pool. It occurred to her that she should have pinned up her hair as she surfaced seconds later, unable to see through its clinging wetness.

'It must be heavy work navigating through this lot,' murmured a deep, masculine voice at her ear, and she felt hands vying with hers in her hair.

Then she felt those hands on her hips, lightly supporting her as she attempted to tread water while struggling to smooth back the suffocating curtain of hair.

'Dip your head under and fling it all back from your face,' advised Paul, his shadowed face close to hers as the brief dusk darkened towards night.

Aggie had obviously yet to get around to reminding Alphonse about the pool lights, thought Sally with a pang of alarm, and immediately ducked under water and began swimming from his grasp. She was brought to an abrupt and protesting halt as a hand circled her ankle and began drawing her back.

'What the hell are you trying to do—drown me?' she choked in fury, inelegantly attempting to tread water with her free leg as he hung tenaciously on to the other.

'I'm afraid of the dark,' he chuckled, pulling her sharply towards him till her thighs straddled his hips.

'Scared the bogeyman will drown you?' she demanded sarcastically, unnerved by the sudden intimacy of their contact.

She damn well would drown him, she vowed as that irritatingly complacent chuckle of his reached her ears, and, placing her hands on his shoulders, she pushed down with all the force she could muster.

All that happened was that her hands slipped against the glistening wetness of his skin and his face, through absolutely no fault of his, became buried in the generous swell of her breasts.

'Get out of there!' she shrieked, as his lips and tongue began to explore, sending shock waves of pleasure coursing through her.

'I can't,' he murmured apologetically. 'Seems the bogeyman's got me.' His shoulders heaved with silent laughter as his mouth resumed its exploration.

Sinking her fingers into the wet gleam of his hair, she attempted to tug him away and was dismayed to find herself sorely tempted to do just the opposite.

'Now what are you doing?' she yelled in alarm, her unconvincing attempts to free herself forgotten as she struggled to see past his nestling head to what his teeth were up to.

They were firmly clamped on her bikini top, and all it took was the single tug he gave for the front-opening clasp to snap free.

'Stop it! You can't do that!' she gasped as his hands slid up her body to cradle the silvery paleness of her breasts. 'What are you doing?' Her words were a shivered croak of uncertainty as pleasure blotted out all thoughts of escape.

It didn't matter that she could see little in the shadowed coolness of the water; her body was telling her with a savage, burgeoning force of the effect of those caressing, kneading hands on it.

'What am I doing, Sally?' he asked huskily, slipping her body lower against his till their faces were level. 'That's quite some question, and at the moment I haven't the answer.'

The touch of his lips was as achingly familiar as it had been that first time. But this time the demand was more urgent, more insistent, and to Sally, as her lips parted in welcoming response to that potent demand, there was as little will to resist as there had been before.

Her long, slim legs wound themselves round his, though all the support she needed was there in the arms holding her closely against the length of that tautly muscled body. Holding her so close that her breasts were aching with the tense, excited awareness of flesh against flesh, and so close that the unmistakable strength of his arousal ignited a corresponding surge of need in her, melting her to him while her arms clung and her body imparted the message of its longing to his.

When his lips parted from hers, they left behind them the softly swollen imprint of their passion, and moved down her body, an impatient heat against her skin as he lifted her higher from the water to bury his face once more against her breasts.

Where initially his mouth had teased and searched, now his teeth were a hungry, rasping presence against the swelling tautness of her flesh, and Sally gave a soft groan of acquiescence as she felt the thrusting search of his tongue on a desire-hardened nipple. She cradled the dark wetness of his head against her, raining frantic, mindless kisses in the damp thickness of his hair as his

mouth sent shivers of excitement coursing through her
till she felt she would explode from the unbearable
tension of longing filling her.

When the underwater lights silently blazed to life, she
heard Paul's throaty groan of protest. Then there was
the fleeting glimpse of the black, curling wetness of his
hair against her skin, the deep tan of his cheek against
the whiteness of her breast before he pulled them both
below the surface of the water.

When they emerged they were in shallower water, and
now that she could stand she found her nose only reached
his breastbone. His hands still held her, resting lightly
on her hips, though their bodies were now several inches
apart.

When she looked up into his face, she felt an increased surge of the desire that had refused to leave her.
The water had grouped the long black lashes of his eyes
into thick, star-like clusters, accentuating the sensuous
message in a gaze that was now a languorous, smoky
blue.

His fingers played against her skin beneath the water,
bringing a choking gasp to the already gulping breath
she was so desperately trying to control.

'Much as I can't wait to make love to you, I do think
we should find somewhere more suitable,' he murmured
huskily, his hands sliding up her body to cup her breasts
once more.

Sally hesitated, mesmerised by his tantalising touch,
her mind reeling from her need to comply with his words.

There had never been a time when she had not been
ultimately in control of her body. With Mark, there had
been times when she had been tempted to give in to
passion, but it had been a temptation she had had little
difficulty resisting. Her body had always seemed to be

governed by an inexplicable need to have no choice; a subconscious conviction that a time would come when her heart would dictate and where there would be no question of choice. It had been a strange perverseness from which she had longed to rid herself, and often she had tried to tell herself how foolish she was being, when Mark was the man she loved and would one day marry. Though she had been glad of her reservations in retrospect, it now hit her squarely how irrational they had been. Given different surroundings, she knew in her heart of hearts that there would have been no choice where this man was concerned—a man she barely knew, let alone loved.

She took a step back, away from the drug of his touch, silently shaking her head in denial of the urgent demands still pulsating through her body.

'No—you don't want to find somewhere more suitable?' he asked quietly, his eyes narrowing to slits as they regarded her.

'No... I don't want to make love,' she whispered raggedly.

'Your terminology is at fault, mermaid. You may not *choose* to make love, but you sure as hell *want* to.'

With a sudden, twisting lunge he left her, powerful kicks from long, bronzed legs propelling his body away with an explosive speed. And his body was still churning back and forth down the pool long after she had slipped into her robe and entered the house.

So much for the mythical effects of a cold shower, she told herself resignedly as she later blow-dried her hair. To think that only a few days ago she had actually rejoiced over having responded to this man!

She gazed gloomily at her reflection as she swept up her hair and secured it. The fact that she could so easily have ended up in bed with him—the mere thought of which set her pulses racing, she observed with a fatalistic resignation—was the least of her troubles. There was still the fact that Jonathan Wincombe was staying at Jacaranda Pools, and the nightmare subterfuge that would doubtless involve her in.

The hopelessness on her face changed to grim determination. There was no point wingeing about being unable to cope, she informed herself sharply. She would damn well have to cope if Zambezi Safaris was to survive.

She smoothed down the folds of the navy caftan she had slipped on, wondering how long the cooling aftermath of her prolonged shower would last, then, with a shrug, she padded barefoot to the kitchen. The aroma of grilling steak wafted to her nostrils, though it did little to arouse her appetite.

'Aggie, I told you I'd cook. I thought you and Alphonse were off to...oh!'

'Oh? I assure you I'm capable of cooking a couple of steaks—how do you like yours?' Paul Morrant, fork in hand, was inspecting the contents of the grill pan.

He had changed, substituting a pair of denims for his swimming trunks, though she could hardly have said he was dressed—the jeans were all he wore.

'Medium verging on well done,' she replied, opening the cutlery drawer and rummaging around in it as she attempted to bring the sudden hammering of her pulse-rate to a semblance of control.

'And what the hell's that supposed to mean?' he demanded with a pained expression.

'Pink in the middle,' she called over her shoulder as she went to lay the table.

Though she was still having problems with her pulse, she gave an involuntary grin at the ripe string of oaths her comment brought.

'I've also knocked up some tomato and onion salad to go with the potato salad,' he informed her as she returned to fetch wine glasses.

'Quite the accomplished chef, aren't you?' she murmured, searching for a bottle opener.

'The wine's already opened,' he pointed out testily. 'And, yes—it's amazing what one can tackle when burdened by a surfeit of energy.'

'What are all the white bits with the tomato salad?' she asked, regretting her sarcasm—responsible though he was for her disturbed pulse, it was unfair to take it out on him. But she determinedly ignored the loaded remark with which he had retaliated. 'Are they almond flakes?' she queried, peering at the salad.

'Garlic . . . I should have warned you, I'm very partial to garlic.'

'Partial? God, we'll send people scuttling at half a mile if we eat that lot!'

'Then we'll only have each other to get close to . . . and won't that be cosy?' he murmured, removing a steak from the grill. 'You realise my steak will ruin while I wait for yours to frazzle,' he remarked, his eyes mocking as they slowly scanned her from head to foot.

'I don't want it frazzled,' she snapped and, aware that the coldness of her tone was definitely not reflected in the heightened colour of her cheeks, she picked up both salads and marched to the dining-room with them.

'Sally, there's no need to be embarrassed by what happened in the pool,' he told her, following her in with the steaks.

'I'm not embarrassed,' she protested, mortified by the colour now flooding her face. 'It's just that . . . we have a sort of business relationship. . . and that's the way I feel it should remain.'

'Wine?'

She nodded, galled to find herself so rattled in the face of such composure. He hadn't been nearly as composed in the pool a while ago, she reminded herself with juvenile relish, and immediately wished she hadn't.

'I could call you Miss Hughes by day, if you like. . . and make love to you only out of business hours,' he offered in tones of innocence she found particularly galling.

'Would you mind dropping this subject?' she asked coldly, hurling a helping of potato salad on to her plate and cursing under her breath as a large portion of it splattered across the highly polished table surface.

'Only if you explain to me why it riles you so. . . you've missed a bit,' he added, considerately spearing the offending morsel on his fork and depositing it on her plate.

'It doesn't rile me!' she exclaimed angrily, while a demon inside her wondered what his reaction would be to the truth—that she resented the powerful physical attraction it was pointless denying she felt towards him, and resented it largely because the risk of becoming emotionally involved with the man she must deceive was one she dared not take.

It was more a certainty than a risk, she realised with a jolt of fear as her eyes met the teasing warmth in his **and her heart automatically turned a somersault.**

'I just happen to be in love with someone else,' she lied defensively.

'Not good enough, mermaid,' he chuckled, the soft, throaty sound sending a shiver through her. 'I only consider married women taboo.'

'Really? And what about engaged women?' demanded Sally, and immediately wished she had had the sense to ignore his comment.

'If an engaged woman responds to me the way you did just now, I'd say she should disengage herself with haste.'

'I've given you my reasons, and if they don't satisfy you, that's your tough luck,' she muttered, her eyes firmly on her plate.

'Well, I shan't force my attentions on you, but don't indulge in horseplay with me unless you're prepared to accept the inevitable. The idea of endlessly prowling the kitchen, knocking up culinary delights as a means of assuaging frustration, doesn't appeal in the least. Especially when you don't even bother to sample the bloody things,' he added, pointedly passing her the tomato salad. 'And try not to sling it all over the table.'

She caught his eye as she took the dish, and despite herself a grin crept to her lips. 'Actually, I sampled some earlier,' she admitted, helping herself to more. 'And it's delicious—as is the steak.'

'I could lie and tell you I'm a culinary genius—but grilling a steak and providing a bit of salad is as far as my gifts go—so I wouldn't advise pushing your luck.'

It took Sally a great deal of mental exertion and an inordinate amount of concentration on her food before she could begin to extricate her senses from the stomach-churning effect of the smile that had accompanied those last words.

She found herself wondering at her own colossal naïveté in her earlier reaction to him. Though even then, she remembered, she had been aware of a positive element of danger in him . . . and that had been from a position of relative safety—before fate had saddled her with his constant presence and the knowledge of just how irresistible his attraction could be.

'By the way...that place in Kabwe—you never got round to telling me if you knew of it,' he remarked suddenly, the familiar shrewd detachment returning to his eyes.

'Yes,' she managed, praying she would escape choking on the mouthful she was struggling to swallow. 'I do know of it. But a lot of those places round Kabwe aren't on the phone,' she lied with disquieting ease. 'Look, I know you're pushed for time, but I'll have to tie up a few loose ends in the office tomorrow. Two of our senior guides start interviewing for staff replacements in a couple of days and I'll have to organise the paperwork. Then I could make a few enquiries and we could perhaps drive up to Kabwe. It's only about sixty miles.'

'What enquiries do you intend making, and of whom?' he demanded with a brusqueness that set her nerves jangling in alarm. He always adopted that rather curt tone when he was discussing business, she reminded herself quickly, and she would end up a nervous wreck if she started reading suspicion into his every utterance.

'You're the one always droning on about discretion,' she reminded him tartly as she evaded answering his question. 'When I've decided to whom I should speak and what I need to say, perhaps you would feel happier if I adopted a foreign accent.'

The eyebrows rose a fraction. They were the most expressive she had ever come across, she decided as the remoteness left his face to be replaced by a slow, curving smile.

'I'd be a lot happier right now if you put on some coffee.'

They took their coffee on to the veranda, though it was still quite a bit hotter there than in the house.

'Would you mind if I smoked a cigar?' asked Paul.

She shook her head. 'I rather like the smell. Perhaps you'd like a cognac,' she suggested as he slipped a case, dull with the gleam of gold, from his back pocket.

He gave her a sidelong glance of amusement as he nodded, then extracted a cigar from the case and began lighting it from the tall flame of a gold Dunhill.

The amusement still lingered on his face when she returned and handed him a brandy balloon.

'Aren't you joining me?'

Sally shook her head and busied herself pouring more coffee. His effect on her was potent enough without alcohol adding to it. And, judging by the permanent expression of amusement his face seemed to have adopted, he was probably quite aware of that unfortunate fact, she thought crossly as she slid his filled cup towards him and glowered across the table at him.

'Stop scowling,' he admonished with a throaty chuckle, then tilted back his head and proceeded to blow a series of smoke rings. 'That's better,' he murmured, as amusement battled with exasperation on her face and eventually won.

Gradually, and with surprising ease, they slipped into companionable conversation. And more and more Sally found herself resenting the constant vigil forced on part of her mind to guard against their conversation veering towards his reasons for being here. The thought of being able to relax completely and just be her true self was one she found exceptionally appealing, and it only heightened the growing strength of her resentment.

Later she took an acidity reading of the pool.

'Alphonse is colour-blind,' she explained as he watched, intrigued, while she took samples of the water and added a few drops of chemical to each. 'It was only when we began having problems with algae that Dad and Jonas realised the problem—Alphonse couldn't interpret these colour-coded tests.'

'That side of it looks far too technical for me,' he laughed. 'But if there's any donkey-work I can do...'

'There is,' she grinned, and handed him a container of chlorine. 'Four scoops... and don't dump it all in the one place.'

She sat on the steps of the veranda and, as she watched him clown around the poolside, laughing as he chucked the measures of chlorine into the water, her eyes seemed to see a Greek god silhouetted in the silver glow of the moon, and she remembered that those gods of old had always winged their way back to Olympus, leaving behind them their careless trail of heartache and havoc on the earth they had fleetingly visited.

CHAPTER FIVE

'MARK? It's Sally.'

'Sally, darling, I've been...'

'Is Jonathan Wincombe at your place?' interrupted Sally, more puzzled than relieved that, after all this time, her sole reaction to that familiar voice was irritation at his use of an endearment. 'Mark? Is he with you?' she demanded as all she heard was his sharply expelled breath.

'No... Sally, we have to talk.' There was an uncharacteristic pleading in Mark Shelby's tone.

'You're damn right we have to talk! What the hell do you think you're up to, Mark? Don't you realise what you...'

'Sally,' he pleaded hoarsely. 'Can you come up here... now?'

'No, I can't,' she exclaimed impatiently. 'I've Wincombe's boss at my place...'

'Morrant!' groaned Mark.

'I'm glad you recognise the name, and I take it you'll know precisely why he's breathing down my neck.'

'Darling, I'm sorry... it's vital that we talk.'

'Mark, where *is* Jonathan Wincombe?'

'Hang on a minute—please, Sally.'

There was a muffled silence as he placed his hand over the receiver, and Sally's fingers began drumming impatiently on her desk top as she waited, trying to quell her mounting alarm. She had left the house early, having begged Aggie not to make the slightest noise that might waken Paul Morrant—the longer he slept, the better. She had also asked the housekeeper to ring and warn her should Paul leave the house. Not that Aggie would have much chance getting through with the phone uselessly engaged as it was now, she thought grimly and glowered at the silent receiver.

'Sally? I could meet you half-way. Can you manage that?'

She agreed—at least there would be no likelihood of her running into Paul Morrant.

She had driven less than twenty-five miles up the Great North Road towards Kabwe when a police Land Rover, coming from the opposite direction, began giving long blasts on its horn.

Immediately she pulled over to the side of the road, watching in alarm as the Land Rover took a screeching 'U' turn and drew up beside her.

Her eyes widened in mystification as Mark Shelby reached out a hand to her from the police vehicle.

'Your car keys, Sally,' he demanded abruptly.

Her hand shaking, she complied then watched as the familiar figure stepped down and into her car. With the same mixture of puzzlement and relief to which she had reacted to the sound of his voice, she realised her concern for Mark was only relative to the effect his problems might have on Zambezi Safaris.

'I had to give him your keys—it was the only way he'd agree to our talking in private,' muttered Mark as the vehicle drew away and parked a few yards ahead of them.

'Mark, what in heaven's name is going on?' she demanded.

Although it was more than a year since she had last seen him, his appearance shocked her. The fact that he was badly in need of a shave might account for an il-

lusion of gauntness about him, she reasoned uncomfortably, but it could in no way account for the heavy
darkness beneath his eyes. The growing, yet irrational,
fear in her that whatever trouble he was in boded ill for
Zambezi Safaris left no room in her heart for pity as she
waited for him to speak.

'I've spent half the night being interrogated by Special
Branch—question after question about Wincombe. God
alone knows what he's been up to, they gave very little
away.'

'Mark, are you under arrest?'

'No,' he replied, his face puzzled as he rasped his
fingers nervously against the stubble on his chin. 'At
least they tell me I'm not. I'm under surveillance for my
own protection—whatever that's supposed to mean.
Wincombe might be a nutcase, but he's hardly dangerous.' He reached out to clasp her hand, which she immediately removed. 'Sally, the guy detailed to guard me
today happens to be an old footballing acquaint-
ance...I've a feeling he's sticking his neck out letting
us meet like this, so for God's sake don't tell a soul.'

Sally nodded, stunned. Just the mention of Jonathan
Wincombe's name had been enough to compound her
fears.

'Mark, where is Jonathan Wincombe?' she repeated,
her words mechanical as she tried to bring a semblance
of order to her thoughts.

He shook his head. 'This is my *ndaba*, love. I don't
want you involved.'

'That's the laugh of the century,' she lashed out in
sudden fury. 'Thanks to your *mind-boggling* stupidity,
I'm totally involved!' Angrily she spelled out her exact
position to him.

Mark's head slumped hopelessly into his hands. 'Sally, none of this was deliberate—I swear to God,' he groaned. 'I hardly know where to begin.'

'I suggest you try,' she informed him coldly.

'Wincombe had approached me on a couple of occasions about starting up a hunting company...it was only after you and I split up that I became interested.' The rueful look he threw her with those last words, Sally merely found irritating. 'Apparently he has an income from a couple of million tied up in investments. He was prepared to stake the lot, he was so keen,' he continued. 'There was an initial problem realising the capital, something to do with his father's will, though that's been sorted out and half of the money has been transferred to the company we formed.'

'Zambezi Trophies.' Sally almost spat the words at him.

'Sally, whatever you may think, certain numbers of animals have to be culled each year...'

'We all know that,' she interrupted coldly. 'It's your deceitful stupidity I find so galling...'

'I admit I wasn't honest. Sally, I'm not blaming you...I know I behaved like a bloody fool. But when you refused to see me, to speak to me on the phone even...I was shattered.'

'So shattered that you tried to destroy Zambezi Safaris?' she asked, her voice deathly quiet.

'Sally, I'd have terminated my contract with Zambezi Safaris before setting up my own company had I had any idea of the backlash there could be,' he vowed.

'And you just happened to use a name similar to ours, and headed paper that was identical in layout and printing to ours?' she accused through clenched teeth.

One look at the bewilderment on his handsome face told her he had absolutely no idea what she was talking about.

'God, how stupid can you be?' she rasped. 'Anyone familiar with Zambezi Safaris' stationery would take one look at yours and assume your outfit was a subsidiary of ours! What on earth possessed you to choose a name so similar?' she demanded in exasperation. 'What possessed you to use our stationery format?'

'Would you believe laziness... and complete lack of imagination?' he asked, his voice hoarse with disbelief. 'Sally, whatever way I look at it... I must have been out of my mind... I respected your father and Jonas, and the last thing I'd want to do is jeopardise the conservation programme. You must believe me, Sally,' he begged.

'I believe you, Mark,' she sighed, wondering what had ever possessed her to believe she had loved this man. 'Mark, don't you think it's about time you got to the point of this meeting?' she added gently.

He turned and looked full into her eyes. Despite his exhaustion, he was still as attractive as ever—still the golden boy—she thought wryly, though her heart felt nothing stronger than a small stab of pity.

'I can't say I ever really took to Wincombe, but I'd no idea he'd turn out to be a complete lunatic,' he muttered, as though speaking to himself, then visibly pulled himself together. 'He took off with Josh Banda a few days ago—we had a couple of elephant licences left over and Wincombe was raring to use them up.' Again he seemed to slip into his own private thoughts. 'Jonas was right. Killing is like a drug to some men, and Wincombe's one of them.' He gave a ragged sigh. 'They're at a small camp up in the Luambe section of Luangwa. I had a radio message from Josh last night, minutes before the police arrived.' He glanced nervously in her direction, then away. 'Wincombe's been badly mauled.'

Sally's head was spinning. 'But the Luangwa Valley park officially closed for the season yesterday. Why on earth are they still in there?' she protested. 'Josh could lose his guide licence...' She stopped, silenced by what she read in his face. 'Mark, why hasn't Josh brought him out?' she asked quietly.

Mark shifted uneasily in the seat. 'Because Josh had to find the leopard and finish it off... Wincombe had wounded it.'

'Leopards don't usually attack people unprovoked...' Sally hesitated; she could feel the colour draining from her face.

'But the bastard tried to convince Josh that it had...even though Josh was near enough to witness him trying to gun down a protected cat.' There was a grim set to his mouth as he turned to face her. 'So you see, not only have I jeopardised your company, but I've formed a partnership with the lowest of the low—a man who would poach a creature as magnificent as a leopard in order to satisfy his bloodlust. I'd turn him in without a second thought, if it weren't for the fact that Josh is unwittingly involved...the poor bloke was half out of his mind with fury when he rang through. It took a lot of self-control on his part not to leave Wincombe for the leopard to finish off.'

'God, what a horrible, unimaginable mess!' she whispered hoarsely.

'Sally, there's more,' stated Mark hollowly. 'They pranged the Land Rover—the radiator's leaking badly. I was on my way up to them with a couple of tins of sealant when the police arrived. I can't go up there with the police nursemaiding me.'

'Is there more?' she groaned.

'Yes—I can't raise them. We've been having problems with the radio on that particular vehicle.'

Sally, whose question had been merely rhetorical, shook her head in total disbelief.

'So, they're stuck in an officially closed game reserve, with a broken-down vehicle and no contact with the outside world?'

Mark nodded miserably.

'For God's sake, Mark! The rains could start any minute now—they could be trapped there for months.'

'I promised Josh I'd get them out without informing the park authorities—he'd lose his licence for sure...and if they got wind of Wincombe's poaching tendencies, you can bet your bottom dollar the little rat would try to involve Josh.'

'If the little rat survives,' pointed out Sally curtly. 'How bad is he?'

'Pretty bad,' muttered Mark morosely.

'You'd better get my keys back,' she informed him wearily. 'It looks as though I have a trip to Luangwa ahead of me.'

'Don't be bloody daft!' exploded Mark. 'I won't let you do it.'

'You won't let me do it?' Her voice was cold with fury. 'Who would you let do it, Mark? One of the Zambezi Safari guides who, along with Josh, would lose his licence if it got out?' she demanded. 'Well, I'm not prepared to ask any of them to take such a risk. All I have to do is follow the map and deliver a couple of cans—which camp is it, precisely?'

She groaned as he named the tiny, probably now derelict, camp.

'It doesn't matter which camp it is,' announced Mark decisively. 'I'll ring the park authorities rather than let you go off alone into that reserve. Sally, it's about the most dangerous...'

'You'll do no such thing,' she interrupted coldly. 'And I shan't be alone. You seem to forget, I have one of the biggest contributors to the conservation programme as my shadow...'

'What the hell's Morrant doing here, anyway?' snapped Mark.

'One of his key employees is missing, for heaven's sake!'

'You can't take him along with you,' he protested. 'Once he sees the set-up, you might just as well kiss the conservation programme goodbye. Besides, you'll need someone who can protect you, not a man who's probably never set foot in the bush before. Sally, please...'

'Will you stop trying to tell me what I can and cannot do?' she interrupted wearily. 'By trying to leave him behind I'd only make him suspicious. I'll just have to come up with a convincing pack of lies. And as for your gallant concern for my safety,' she added, with a touch of malice, 'he may be new to the bush, but somehow I can't envisage Paul Morrant losing his head in an emergency. Satisfied?'

'Of course I'm not satisfied,' he muttered savagely. 'But what can I say?' he added hopelessly.

'Just get me my keys, Mark; there's nothing you can say.'

'Sally, you can't go without a rifle.'

The look she gave him was withering.

'And you'll have to go right up through Lundazi, then south to skirt Mbuzi and any patrols,' he continued undeterred.

'I realise that,' she told him quietly, and once more repeated her request for her keys.

'Where the hell have you been?'

Ignoring his snarled greeting, Sally slipped past a blackly scowling Paul Morrant and into the house.

'Sally!' he bellowed, grasping her by the arm and swinging her round to face him. 'In case it escaped your attention, I'm not here to soak up the sun. I have a business to run!'

'And needless to say you're the *only* person with a business to run. What the hell do you think I've been doing?' she flared. 'You seem to forget—I'm not one of your unfortunate employees.'

'OK—I apologise!' He hesitated, his hectoring tone changing to one of concern as he saw the tense exhaustion on her face. 'Sally...what's wrong?'

'Something's cropped up. Paul, give me a moment to unwind...please. Then I'll explain,' she told him wearily.

'Why don't you have a swim? You look whacked. I'll ask Aggie to make a jug of something cold and refreshing.'

She nodded thankfully, made her way to her room and changed into a bikini.

The fierce heat of the sun had brought the water almost to the temperature of a tepid bath, offering no balm to Sally as she glided back and forth lethargically.

She needed this time to think before she faced Paul. So preoccupied had she been on the journey back from seeing Mark that she had almost knocked down a jay walker and had then driven through a set of traffic lights on red. And still she had not been able to come up with a plausible excuse for the secrecy that would have to surround the trip to the game reserve. Her only hope was to play on Paul's anxiety to get to Jonathan Wincombe as quickly as possible.

A plan gradually formed in her mind—a flimsy one that would no doubt disintegrate under the scrutiny of anyone familiar with the way the Zambian authorities operated. It wasn't exactly brilliant, but it was all she could come up with, she told herself as she stepped wearily from the pool.

'Aggie wants you.' There was an amused grin on Paul's face as he deposited a tray on the veranda table. 'Seems you're in her bad books.'

Frowning, Sally made her way to the kitchen and found Aggie at the far door.

'We'll talk in your bedroom,' beckoned the house-keeper and disappeared.

'Aggie...'

'Close the door,' ordered the woman impatiently. 'Where were you? He tried ringing and there was no reply.'

'I had to see someone.'

'*Bwana* Paul had three visitors—two foreign Europeans—he could speak their language, but I don't know what it was. But I recognised the Zambian with them and he's big...a superintendent in Special Branch. I couldn't hear what they said, as he made me leave the room,' added Aggie with an indignant sniff.

Sally slumped weakly to the bed. It had been Special Branch who had questioned Mark and put a police guard on him, and it was that same élite section of the Zambian police which was always called in where foreign nationals were involved. Yet Paul Morrant had categorically stated he did not want the police involved. She shrugged, completely mystified.

'Thanks for letting me know, Aggie,' she murmured. 'Though I've no idea what it all means. I'd better get back to Paul before he comes looking for me,' she added with an attempt at a grin.

'He already did that,' reported Aggie. 'This morning, after those three left.'

With her heart now firmly settled in her stomach, Sally made her way back to the veranda.

'Still in one piece, I see,' remarked Paul, handing her a glass of fresh orange juice.

For a second she looked puzzled, then mentally kicked herself. 'Aggie's been sharpening her tongue on me for the best part of fourteen years now—that was a mild bout.'

'Have you unwound sufficiently to tell me about your morning?' he asked as she took a sip of the cold drink.

She lowered the glass and placed it on the table with painstaking deliberation.

'Jonathan Wincombe isn't in Kabwe—he's in the Luangwa Valley game reserve.' The words came out in a breathless rush. 'It's all rather complicated,' she added panic surging through her as her mind became a complete blank.

'Perhaps you had better explain,' he stated, his tone ominously quiet.

'They shouldn't be there...you see, the park closed officially yesterday—well, at dusk the night before, to be precise. They didn't get out in time because their radiator sprung a leak.' She was gabbling like a complete idiot, she told herself helplessly, unable to stop.

'And?' he prompted, with uncharacteristic patience.

'My informant...' Now she sounded like a character in a spy novel, she thought in desperation as she struggled to pull herself together. '...he was to sneak in with some radiator sealant...'

'Why would he feel the need to sneak in?' There was steel in his tone.

'Because he'd have to inform the...the police that there were people still in the reserve. The guide with Mr Wincombe would lose his licence.'

'Why?'

Sally took another gulp of juice while trying to unfreeze her mind.

'Because the guide obviously didn't follow the correct procedure on entering the park—otherwise the wardens would have known two people were unaccounted for.' She had, she realised, inadvertently hit on the truth in the midst of her string of lies. Guides entering the parks without clients often cut through the red tape, and she could only suppose Josh no longer regarded Jonathan Wincombe as a client.

'Sally, do you think you could manage to come to the point?' he asked, in tones of ice.

'I told him I'd...we'd take the sealant up there. That way, you'd get straight to your errant employee and retrieve your precious codes,' she informed him waspishly, unable to prevent herself venting a minute part of her pent-up tension on him.

'And how did he react to your suggestion?'

'Gratefully. He didn't relish the idea of traipsing all the way up there, anyway.'

'But he didn't mind letting a slip of a girl go, with a man who's never set foot in this part of Africa before,' he observed.

'I told him you were a safari guide,' she lied. 'Perhaps you'd have felt happier had I told him your true profession,' she added with a flare of anger.

'Your discretion was admirable in the extreme,' he drawled. 'When do we leave?'

'As soon as possible,' she replied, glancing at her watch and resolutely smothering her pique at his dismissive tone. 'There's a rest camp at Lundazi—we should aim for that before nightfall. I'll ask Aggie to make up some sandwiches and a couple of flasks while I change.

Paul's insistence that they take the powerful Mercedes he had hired had met with Sally's voluble resistance.

'How can you consider taking a thing like that into a game park?' she objected. 'Adequate though the road system may be here, there are only dirt tracks in the reserves.'

'Which the car-hire firm claimed the Mercedes is perfectly capable of handling.' His look was infuriatingly complacent. 'Besides, it's faster, more comfortable and, unlike that wreck of yours, is unlikely to shed its exhaust at the first bump we hit. It also happens to be air-conditioned.'

'I'll need to transfer some things to your boot, then,' she muttered with resignation. She knew perfectly well he was right. The only reason she had suggested taking her car, which admittedly looked a mite forlorn beside the smug opulence of his, was because her boot contained the rifle and ammunition she had collected from the company's armoury on her way home.

'Here,' she muttered ungraciously, passing him the two cans of sealant Mark had told her to get.

She had just transferred the rifle to the rear floor of the Mercedes when she became conscious that her actions were being observed through the back window.

'I do know how to use it,' she informed him defensively. 'And it would be madness to go up there without it.'

'Having the obvious pointed out to me is something I find particularly galling—almost as galling as your ludicrous furtiveness,' he commented sharply.

'One way or another, it seems you're in for a pretty galling time of it,' she snapped, flinging the ammunition next to the rifle. She gave a shriek of outrage as she was hauled roughly from the car.

'That's the second time in less than a minute you've managed to state the obvious,' he snarled, his eyes glittering with ice. 'Now it's my turn. Should the need arise, I'll be the one using that rifle—only an idiot would handle ammunition the way you just did!'

Sally opened her mouth to retort, then closed it quickly, silenced as much by the unmistakable anger on his face as by the certain knowledge that his criticism had been more than deserved.

'Why don't you do something useful and see if Aggie's finished the food?' he suggested frostily.

Silently she flounced past him and into the house.

'You two at it again?' beamed Aggie, closing a large, and miraculously laden, insulated bag.

'I don't know what you're looking so happy about,' scowled Sally. 'That man is the most insufferably self-opinionated person I've ever had the misfortune to meet.'

'Is that so? Can't be many girls around who'd describe meeting him as a misfortune,' chuckled Aggie. 'If he's so bad, why are you going off on a picnic with him?'

'For God's sake, Aggie—it's not a picnic! It's all to do with this...this business.'

The housekeeper's face sobered in alarm. 'How long will you be gone?'

'I don't know,' sighed Sally. 'A couple of nights, perhaps. You're not to worry, love.' She gave the woman a quick hug and picked up the bag before she could be faced with further questions.

They had driven for almost two hours with barely a word exchanged, and it was beginning to have the most appalling effect on Sally's mind.

Each inadvertently snatched glimpse of the remote features of the man beside her brought vivid memories of that handsome face transformed by passion. The hands that now held the steering wheel were the same hands that had once caressed her body to a wildness she had never before experienced.

She was going out of her mind, she told herself with fatalistic calm. And it was perfectly understandable. She had had dumped on her shoulders a burden she was mentally incapable of handling, and it was no wonder her mind was giving way—the terrible knowledge of what could well be at stake was an unbearable strain. She had to cope, she told herself frantically, remembering, with a stab of longing, the ease and laughter of the night before. It had been almost like friendship, and it was what she needed most now; without the illusion of comfort it brought, she knew she was in danger of snapping.

'Paul——' she blurted out, even before any words had formed in her mind.

'Sally?'

'I know I bring out the worst in you . . . but I've decided to try not to.'

'You've worked out what causes it, have you?' he enquired with chilling politeness.

'No, I haven't . . . oh, what's the use? It's just me in general.'

'You're wrong. It's particular facets of you I find infuriating.'

'Ha, ha!' she exclaimed mirthlessly, turning her back to him and gazing sightlessly out of the window.

'Well, that attempt at pleasing didn't last very long,' he observed piously.

'It wasn't my intention to please you,' she flared, huddling deep into her seat. 'Just to stop incurring your foul-tempered wrath every time I open my mouth!'

Her words of fury were met with an initial silence, followed by a strange, choking sound.

She peered suspiciously over her shoulder to find him laughing.

'Why not try feeding me a sandwich or two? You'll find the effect miraculous.'

Her desperate need not to be left in silence with her exceedingly disturbing thoughts forced her to comply.

She opened the insulated bag and gasped. 'Aggie's surpassed herself this time! How about some of these?' She extracted sandwiches bulging with home-cooked ham and salad and handed him one. 'There's chicken, too,' she offered. 'How about a drumstick?'

'Just keep the supplies rolling in my direction,' he grinned. With an answering smile, she did exactly that.

'As they say—the way to a man's heart is through his stomach,' he observed later, with an angelic smile, having demolished several sandwiches and a good deal of the chicken.

Seconds later he was frowning and impatiently stabbing at buttons on the dashboard.

'I don't believe it! The damn air-conditioning's packed up!'

'Language, Mr Morrant, please,' she begged primly, and flashed him a mischievous grin. 'Tell me, is that your exhaust I hear rattling?'

'You tell me, Miss Hughes,' he chuckled softly. 'Do you really fancy travelling in the boot?'

An hour later, with the residual coolness from the air-conditioning spent, they were forced to open the windows. But the breeze that drifted in to them was a heavy, enervating waft of humidity that left them limp and bathed in perspiration.

'Even this scenery's enough to make you feel hot, just looking at it,' complained Paul, as they drove through mile after mile of flat, parched bushland. 'I don't think I've ever seen anything quite as arid and desolate as this before.'

'The rains are due any day now—and the transformation they bring is miraculous. This whole place will have a lush greenness you just wouldn't imagine possible, having seen it like this,' Sally told him. 'Mind you, the scenery gets much more interesting the further north we go: hilly and with lots of trees...and lurking elephants!'

Dusk was making its rapid transformation into night as they approached the tiny town of Lundazi.

'It's like something out of one of those old Hollywood cowboy films,' observed Paul drily. 'A ghost town—complete with hitching posts for the horses,' he chuckled, pointing towards the weathered posts propping up wooden awnings along the main street.

'Turn left just up there,' instructed Sally, peering through the quickly waning dusk.

Apart from towering avocado trees that encircled it and provided welcome shade by day, there was little that could be described as inviting about the starkly functional, single-storey hostel in front of which they drew up. It was of the same, almost barrack-like design of about a dozen such places the Zambian Tourist Board had erected in remote areas—where travellers were guaranteed a clean, cheap bed for the night and basic meals all year round. And it *was* all year round, Sally reminded herself noting, with a small stab of alarm, that the place was in darkness.

'Seems the Lundazi Hilton's shut up shop and sent the staff home,' muttered Paul, switching off the engine.

'All the Tourist Board hostels remain open all year round,' Sally assured him, with a confidence she was beginning to doubt.

It took them a good ten minutes of calling and hammering on the door before they raised the disgruntled caretaker.

His English seemed minimal and it took another ten minutes for Sally to get over the message that she would report him to the Zambian Tourist Board, who would undoubtedly fire him, if he refused them accommodation.

'Remind me never to cross you,' murmured her companion appreciatively.

Eventually, and with patent reluctance, the caretaker beckoned them to follow him.

The room into which he led them was small, clean and sparsely furnished. It contained two single beds, both made up, and each had a mosquito net suspended from the ceiling and folded neatly to the back of its headboard.

Sally nodded. 'Where's the other room?' she asked.

The caretaker regarded her blankly.

'We need two rooms. One for him.' She spoke slowly and distinctly, pointing her finger in Paul's direction to stress her point. 'And one for me.' She then held up two fingers and turned, startled, as the banker made a choking sound.

'I think he's under the impression you're making rude signs to him,' he murmured, composing his face to a look of by-standing innocence.

Sally glared at him and returned her attention to the man by now half-way out of the room.

'We need two rooms!' she insisted, running after him.

'Two beds, madam, only one room,' responded the Zambian, his tone uninterested. 'No food, you book too late.'

'Leave it, Sally,' advised a quiet voice from behind her. 'I'll sleep in the car.'

'Of course you can't!' she exclaimed. 'If you open the windows you'll be eaten alive, if you don't you'll swelter.'

'If that's the case, there's something I have to ask you.'

She turned to face him, alarmed by his anxious tone.

'Sally, can I rely on you not to take advantage of me just because we're forced to share a room?'

She gave an indignant groan that gradually turned to laughter—he had an enviable knack of injecting humour into awkward moments, even though his choice of words was hardly comforting.

'See if you can bully the whereabouts of a bathroom out of our genial host, while I get the things from the car,' he suggested, giving her a gentle shove.

The shower facilities turned out to be surprisingly good, with the cold taps providing water only a few degrees above tepid. Feeling as refreshed as she was ever likely to in such enervating heat, Sally decided to take on the caretaker once more. Within minutes she was seething with frustration in the face of his implacable and, she felt certain, deliberate incomprehension.

'Why don't you accept the inevitable and give in gracefully?' suggested a mocking voice.

She turned and glared at the man destined to be her room-mate for the night. His hair still damp from the shower, he looked enviably cool—and infuriatingly untroubled.

'He's being deliberately unhelpful,' protested Sally angrily. 'He's quite capable of understanding English when he chooses.'

'And he obviously doesn't choose now,' observed Paul mildly. 'So why get yourself all steamed up? Come on, we'll see if we can find somewhere to eat.'

Sally bit back an angry retort that they were in the wilds of Africa, not Knightsbridge; instead she followed him out, giving the caretaker a departing glower of outrage.

'I suppose that was Lundazi that was,' remarked Paul laconically as six minutes later they finished their tour of the tiny town.

'We've still a load of Aggie's food left,' chuckled Sally. 'And we can stock up on drinks for tomorrow at that bottle store we passed.'

It was the only place they had passed that showed any sign of life, and the shopkeeper rushed to the door to welcome them, bowing and silently clapping his hands in the traditional greeting to which Sally automatically responded.

To her surprise, her tall companion immediately did likewise. There was no denying that, when he felt inclined, Paul Morrant's social sense was impeccable, she thought in amusement as the beaming shopkeeper proudly displayed his meagre stocks to them. Passing over almost liquid bars of chocolate and the crisps, which had responded to a surreptitious squeeze with all the pliability of rubber, they bought up the entire supply of drinks—ten lagers and a dozen cans of lemonade.

Back in the room, Sally did her utmost to stifle her increasing lack of ease—silently cursing the man, now stretched out on one of the beds, so thoroughly at peace with the world for once.

'Will it be necessary to sleep under that?' he asked lazily, glancing up at the netting. 'There's wire mesh on all the windows.'

'Things have a knack of getting past mesh in these parts. Have you taken anything against malaria?' she demanded anxiously.

He nodded, plainly amused by her tone.

'Even so, it pays to sleep under a net—unless you've no objections to being eaten alive.'

'Talking of eating, I'm starved,' he announced, suddenly rising from the bed. 'It's a pity we have nothing more suitable in which to toast Aggie's culinary skills,' he grinned, picking up two lukewarm beers and handing her one. 'Not to mention our first night together.'

Mortified by the colour she knew had leapt to her cheeks, Sally began racking her mind for a suitably flippant retort. She had still come up with nothing by the time he had seated himself beside her on the second bed and had begun tucking heartily into the food.

'Cosy, isn't it?' he murmured innocently, proffering a piece of chicken.

'Paul, I'm perfectly capable of feeding myself,' she snapped, as he waved it temptingly under her nose.

She took the piece of meat, conscious of the warmth of his body against her side as he leaned casually against her, and began eating mechanically.

She toyed with the idea of moving to the other bed, then discarded it. She had no intention of giving him any hint of the effect his nearness was having on her—though he probably needed none. It was when her mind began drifting relentlessly back once more to their encounter in the pool that she leapt to her feet and began tidying away the remnants of the meal.

'For God's sake, Sally!' he exclaimed, rising and following her. 'Stop being so jumpy—you're making me nervous.' Taking her gently by the shoulders, he turned her round to face him. 'I'm not going to attack you,' he admonished softly, his eyes caressing hers with amusement and rebuke. 'If anything happens between us tonight, it will only be because you want it to happen.'

'I don't think you're a monster,' she whispered, unnerved by the sudden blast of awakening his words had wrought on her body.

'I'm glad to hear that.' The laugh he gave was a low, husky breath that sent her senses reeling, making her oblivious of the fact that his hands had slid up her shoulders and were now lightly clasping her neck. 'I have a couple of phone calls to make.' His thumbs moved hypnotically at the base of her neck. 'So perhaps you'd better turn in. We have an early start ahead of us.'

Sally nodded, unable to speak.

'Goodnight, Sally.'

By the time she had collected her wits sufficiently to reply, it was too late. She was responding in a way that seemed to come as second nature to her, to the lips that bent and claimed hers. Her arms reached out to clasp and welcome him as the now familiar longing possessed her, betraying itself in the answering hunger of her mouth beneath his.

'Sally, there are goodnight kisses and goodnight kisses,' he groaned, suddenly wrenching his mouth from hers. 'And I've an uncomfortable feeling I'm getting the wrong message from this particular one.'

He cupped her face in his hands and drew her away from him, giving a husky sigh of a laugh as he gazed down at her. 'God knows, there are times when you do bring out the worst in me,' he whispered hoarsely. 'But it appears you can also bring out the best...I really do have some phone calls to make, and I'm going now...before I revert to type.'

In a complete daze, Sally watched him go. Then she returned to the bed and sank heavily down on it.

She barely knew the man, she told herself while trying to unravel her mind. Scarcely a week ago he had been no more than an aggressively abusive voice on the end of a phone. And now, all he had to do was touch her and her mind refused to function...while her body behaved in a way that was completely alien to her. Distractedly she jumped to her feet and began lowering the netting over both beds.

She was letting the wretched predicament she was in take over her life—affect her judgement—and it was a quick way to losing her sanity, she told herself firmly.

The fact that she found him so attractive naturally complicated things. And probably the fact that she knew she could not afford to explore that attraction somehow perversely increased its effect. All she had to do was keep things in perspective, and a close watch on herself.

Her eyes rested on the bed she had just finished preparing—his bed—and, with an exclamation of impatience with herself, she began undressing.

Determined to blank her mind, she slipped into a loose T-shirt and a pair of briefs—two items of clothing she could well do without in heat like this, she thought discontentedly—then switched off the light and made her way through the gap she had left in the tucked-in netting.

Still battling with her constantly straying mind, she silently cursed the mosquito netting as she painstakingly tucked the rest under the mattress. Vital though they might be in this area, she loathed them. It was like sleeping in a heat-producing shroud—not that she was likely to be blessed by sleep...

CHAPTER SIX

SALLY'S eyes began to open as the first fingers of a crimson dawn threaded their threat of heat across the skies. She scrambled her way out of the airless cocoon of netting, her sleep-dazed mind struggling to orient itself to unfamiliar surroundings.

Seated on the edge of the bed, she gradually got her bearings and was immediately struggling to ward off the unsettling thoughts that accompanied her full awakening.

Her eyes strayed to the still sleeping form on the second bed, and she quashed the sudden leap of her heart with a sigh of exasperation. So much for the painstaking trouble she had taken with his net, she thought irritably; the long, lean body, naked save for a pair of boxer shorts, was completely uncovered.

Her eyes proved curiously reluctant to leave that body, lying flat on its stomach, head pillowed on clasped arms, and she found herself wondering in what part of the world the sun had darkened its skin to so deep a golden brown.

With an exclamation of impatience she dragged her eyes away, tartly informing herself that she had warned him of the consequences of not sleeping under a net.

She showered, then dressed, and found herself wondering if he had really had phone calls to make the night before and, if so, who it was he had needed to ring...not that she could possibly ask. No wonder she had been acting so irrationally, she thought despairingly, when she was terrified of opening her mouth in case she carelessly said the wrong thing or let something slip. Her mind refused point-blank to consider what might lie ahead when they eventually reached the camp, instead it began a niggling protest at the thought of the breakfast that lay ahead. Wilting sandwiches and warm lemonade, she told herself in disgust as she opened the bathroom door and found her nostrils assailed by the unbelievable aroma of fresh coffee.

Telling herself she was dreaming, she nevertheless followed her nose and found herself in a small kitchen.

'Good morning, madam. I am Jeremiah, the day warden.'

Sally returned the bow and hand-clapping of the smiling, wizened man who had spoken.

'I have made breakfast for you and the *Bwana*.'

Sally could only beam her incredulous delight. She watched as the warden retrieved six hot, crisp rolls and transferred them to a plaited basket on a tray. Apart from the basket, the tray held a dish of butter and another containing a section of fresh honeycomb.

'I'll take this to your room,' grinned Jeremiah, lifting the tray.

Paul was sitting on the edge of his bed, wearing only a pair of close-fitting lightweight cotton jeans and a night's growth of dark stubble.

The incipient beard lent him a rakish, almost carefree look, except that his eyes were heavy-lidded and peculiarly dulled, as though he had reached the point of total exhaustion.

'This is Jeremiah, our fairy godfather,' announced Sally, brightness masking her alarm at his appearance.

'Good morning, Jeremiah,' he murmured, rising to his feet. 'Is that actually coffee, or am I dreaming?'

'No dream, *Bwana*, just very good coffee,' grinned the warden happily as the towering Englishman relieved him of his tray and placed it on Sally's bed.

'I must say Jeremiah's a vast improvement on last night's character,' he remarked, liberally buttering a roll and adding a dollop of honey.

Sally nodded and began pouring the coffee, still disturbed by his appearance.

'Paul...are you OK? You look a bit rough.'

'I'll be fine when I've had a shave. God, it was like being in a sauna under that wretched netting.'

'Except that you weren't under it,' she pointed out with a wry smile. 'You must have been eaten alive.'

He shook his head, his mouth full of honeyed roll.

'I don't believe you,' she laughed, as he sat down beside her on his bed and drained his cup.

'Disappointed?' he enquired mockingly, holding out his cup to her for a refill.

'If you want more, you know where the pot is,' she informed him tartly, ignoring his remark.

'God, but you're going to make some poor devil a rotten wife,' he remarked as he filled his cup. 'Would you like more?' he added angelically, and took her proffered cup.

'You've definitely been taking something for malaria, have you?' probed Sally. His eyes looked ghastly.

'I was supposed to be taking part in a yacht race in **Mombasa—this week, in fact**. So—yes, I've very definitely being taking the necessary. Satisfied?'

'What a hard life you busy merchant bankers have,' murmured Sally sarcastically, stung by his tone.

'We do indeed,' he replied, deadpan. 'And many of us play as hard as we work, though, personally, I don't believe in mixing the two. And, as this happens to be just another working day, I suggest we get a move on.'

Sally was almost choking on her roll in her haste to get it swallowed and give him a piece of her mind when she noticed him rubbing at his neck.

He was still rubbing as he made his way to the door.

'If it's any consolation, I think something's been having a go at my jugular,' he announced wanly as he turned and faced her.

Sally frowned as she saw a reddened, blotchy patch trailing down his neck to the curve of his shoulder. 'Don't scratch it,' she warned. 'It could...'

'Stop acting like a mother hen—it doesn't suit you,' he drawled. 'Besides, I'm not scratching—it doesn't itch.'

He could damn well sleep under a tree from now on for all she cared, thought Sally furiously as he sauntered from the room.

Her anger had long since dissipated itself as they approached the game park—to be replaced by growing apprehension. She was wondering just how much she should tell him of the dangers that lay ahead, while a part of her was constantly being distracted by the certainty that he was unwell.

'I don't know why you won't let me drive—you still look terrible.'

'So you seem to delight in telling me,' he retorted irritably.

'We've just entered the boundaries of the park proper,' she pointed out, determined not to lose her temper.

'OK,' he conceded, halting the car. 'You drive and I'll ride shotgun.'

Before Sally could speak, he was out of the car, retrieving the rifle and loading it.

She slid over to the driver's seat, her expression grim as she watched him re-enter and casually place the loaded weapon within easy reach on the back seat. The flippancy of his remark had made her wonder if he had any idea at all of the enormity of what they were undertaking.

Fear snapped her patience. 'Have you any conception of the possible dangers ahead?' she demanded.

'If there's something you feel you should tell me, I suggest you go ahead—though some might think your timing was a little suspect,' he informed her laconically.

'Perhaps I gave you more credit than you deserve,' snapped Sally. 'But I'll spell it out now. We're illegally entering possibly one of the most dangerous places in the entire continent—and I don't only mean because of the animals. If anything happens, there will be no patrols to come and get us.'

'A fact of which I'm perfectly aware.'

She wondered if she should tell him that the only patrol they were likely to come across would be an anti-poaching unit, whom bitter experience had taught to disable first and ask questions in safety after. The fact that they were entering an area unfavoured by poachers, and therefore unlikely to be patrolled, kept her quiet— the less she had to tell him the better.

'Sally, I understand your fears,' he told her quietly, his tone devoid of sarcasm for once. 'And I promise you I'm quite reliable in an emergency—so, how about getting us under way?'

The lethargy that had worried her earlier seemed to have left him as they drove at snail's pace along the rutted single-width track, and she was relieved to see he seemed perfectly relaxed. His fascinated absorption in their surroundings became total as a herd of kudu skipped across their path, the vertical white stripes on their flanks gleaming against the red-brown of their hides. There was delight on his face as he watched the agile springing leaps of the smaller, similarly coloured impala, sweeping by. But it was the elegant, sway-necked giraffes who entranced him most as they gazed benignly down at them from their great heights.

'Those are what I'd really call eyelashes,' he chuckled, as one giraffe bent its head to investigate them, peering unconcernedly at them through liquid brown eyes ringed with comically long lashes.

Several times they were brought to a halt by jay-walking warthogs, their perpendicular tails standing to stiff attention as they darted across the track, snorting and bickering among themselves. Again they slowed to a halt as a herd of buffalo crossed in front of them, the huge bull pawing the ground in a half-hearted ritual challenge before sauntering off.

'A surprisingly mild buffalo,' observed Sally with a small sigh of relief.

'And if he hadn't been?' questioned Paul.

'I'd have held my ground and prayed. They usually only make a few dummy charges, though they've been known to dent a few bumpers. As with elephant, the last thing you do is back off—they feel they have the upper hand then.'

'It's comforting to know I'm in such capable hands,' he chuckled.

'What would you have done . . . had he charged?'

'I'd probably have called his bluff and driven towards him.'

'I can't think of a better way of getting a car written off,' laughed Sally.

'Which is why we're both probably much safer with you at the wheel.'

'Probably?' murmured Sally, inordinately relieved that his early-morning lethargy now seemed completely gone.

'Merely a slip of the tongue—I meant to say positively.'

The air was filled with the incessant shrill of cicadas as they moved from parched open planes into densely wooded jungle.

'What on earth caused that?' demanded Paul as they passed through an area of total destruction, where huge trees had been stripped of their barks and bleached a ghostly silver-grey by the sun and where smaller ones had been up-rooted completely.

'Elephant,' Sally told him. 'They're very partial to the barks of certain trees, and demolish them completely.'

Seconds later there was no trace of lethargy in either of them as they rounded a corner and into the midst of a herd of meandering elephants.

'God, but they're magnificent!' breathed Paul, awe-struck. 'They're the size of small houses.'

Sally switched off the ignition as more of the herd appeared, this time to the back of the car.

They were now completely surrounded by an ambling mass of grey and it was several minutes before the herd, over a hundred in all, passed. Sally was just about to switch on the engine once more when a huge tusker lumbered into their path.

'He looks as though he means business,' murmured Paul in total fascination, as the huge animal threw up its trunk and shrilled a blast of rage at them.

Sally watched, her hand hovering helplessly on the ignition key, as the elephant took a few shuffling steps in reverse then billowed out its ears and charged.

The huge animal stopped barely three feet short of the Mercedes. It ambled back to where it had been, then charged again. On its third rush, it stopped only inches short of the car, and it was then that Paul reached back for the rifle.

'I'm entirely in your hands, Sally,' he told her quietly. 'Any suggestions?'

'If he charges with his ears flattened back, I'm afraid we'll have no choice,' she whispered hoarsely. 'But only if he flattens back his ears.'

The bull elephant charged them twice more, each time stopping only a nerve-racking inch or two away from the bonnet of the car. On neither occasion did Paul Morrant raise the rifle slung across his knees.

'I think I could do with a lemonade,' croaked Sally as the elephant decided he had had enough fun for the day and ambled off. 'Thank you for not panicking when most would have,' she breathed gratefully as he handed her a can.

'Seems I have more faith in you than you have in me,' he observed drily. 'That was a useful tip about the ears.'

'They flap their ears to frighten you,' she told him as he took the can from her and drank the remainder. 'Once they stop, they're not bothered whether you're scared or not—they're after you. Perhaps what I should have said was thanks for trusting me,' she added quietly and started up the car.

Paul made no comment, but for several seconds she was conscious of his eyes on her, and they spent the two hours it took them to reach their destination in a silence broken only by the cries and calls of the bush that surrounded them and a background of chirping, cricket-like cicadas and sweltering heat.

They drew up in a sun-scorched clearing on which stood three small *rondavels*, the round, thatched-roofed huts that served as sleeping quarters, out of one of which stumbled an almost unrecognisably subdued and weary Josh Banda.

Paul leapt from the car and approached him.

'Where's Wincombe?' he demanded.

Josh indicated the *rondavel* from which he had come. 'He's in a pretty bad way,' he muttered and continued towards the car, his face troubled. 'Sally, I swear to God I didn't know he'd stoop to poaching,' he blurted out unhappily.

'Of course you didn't,' Sally consoled him, getting out of the car. 'But not a word of that to Mr Morrant,' she begged, clutching him by the arm.

The tall, thick-set Zambian gave a groan of agony at her touch.

'Josh, what is it? Oh, my God!' she gasped as she caught sight of an ominous dark stain on the sleeve of his dark green safari jacket. Then her eyes travelled to where the sleeve had been ripped open to expose an angry, gaping wound.

'Josh!'

'It happened when Wincombe nearly wrote off the Land Rover. That man's a jinx...'

'Sally!' Paul was beckoning her from the door of the *rondavel*. With a quick warning squeeze on Josh's hand, Sally went to join him.

The inside of the hut was almost cool in comparison to the heat that shimmered relentlessly outside, and it was several seconds before Sally's eyes adjusted to the darkness of her surroundings. Two camp cots, two rough wooden chairs and a small table took up most of the floor space in the small circular room. On one of the two beds lay Jonathan Wincombe, his face an unhealthy yellow beneath the stubble of beard and sheen of perspiration, his breathing a hoarse, laboured rasp.

'I've been sponging him down every fifteen minutes in an attempt to reduce the fever,' remarked Josh wearily from behind her. 'But his breathing got like this within the last hour.'

'We'll have to get him to a hospital as quickly as possible,' muttered Paul, as Sally prayed he would not draw back the sheet Josh had laid over the man—by no stretch of anyone's imagination could a mauling from a leopard be mistaken for injuries sustained in a minor crash.

Paul moved away from the bed. 'The poor devil's in a pretty bad state.' He turned to Josh. 'We'd best go and retrieve that Land Rover and get him out of here as quickly as we can.' Sally heaved a sigh of relief as the two men left, then drew back the sheet from the unconscious man and had to stifle a groan of horror.

Josh had stripped the man and obviously done the best he could to clean the savage claw marks that had slashed open the body. The wounds looked remarkably clean, she noted as she anxiously examined them one by one—there were only a couple ringed with the ominous red puffiness of infection.

She noticed a large, empty antiseptic bottle on the floor next to a small first-aid box—at least Josh had had something to help stave off infection, she realised thankfully.

Quickly she rifled through the box, ripping open packets of sterile lint and placing them over the wounds, loosely bandaging them in place round his legs and, unwilling to disturb him by attempting to lift him, using sticking plaster where she could on his body.

At least he would be that bit more comfortable on the journey, she told herself when she had finished. And Paul Morrant would be unable to see the wounds should he look, added a guilty inner voice.

'We'll have to get Wincombe into the Mercedes.'

Sally started as she heard Paul's voice at the door.

'Josh can follow us later, when he's seen to the radiator,' he added.

Sally shook her head. 'Josh had better take him,' she stated firmly, as the Zambian joined him at the door. 'He needs medical treatment just as badly as Wincombe. Haven't you noticed the state his arm's in?' she demanded as Josh immediately began shaking his head.

Paul took one look at the arm the man had obviously deliberately kept concealed from him and handed him the keys. 'It's an automatic, so it shouldn't put too much strain on that arm of yours,' he told him with surprising gentleness. 'Sally and I shouldn't be too far behind.'

Josh shook his head again. 'That sealant has to be left for at least twelve hours before the radiator can be filled,' he pointed out.

Paul shrugged. 'It seems we haven't much choice— we leave the Land Rover and the four of us go in the car.'

Josh's lips tightened stubbornly. 'I can't leave that vehicle here . . . once it's discovered and traced back to me, I'll lose my guide permit.' His eyes pleaded as they met Sally's. 'I'll stay on my own and follow tomorrow.'

'An injured man, alone in this place?' exclaimed Paul impatiently. 'I shan't hear of it! The authorities are bound to make some allowances for the fact that Wincombe was injured . . .'

'I'm staying,' repeated the Zambian implacably.

'No, you're not,' rasped Sally, rounding on him impatiently. She knew Josh Banda well enough to know he had probably used none of the stock of antiseptic on himself. He was likely to be in far more danger from infection than Wincombe, and forcefully told him so.

'Paul and I will stay and bring out the Land Rover,' she told him, ignoring the Englishman's look of surprise. 'Josh, you know as well as I do that you could end up losing that arm if you got held up getting back...how many one-armed guides do you know of?'

'For God's sake!' exclaimed Paul. 'Could we settle this once and for all? I'll stay. Now—let's get Wincombe into the car.'

Both Sally and Josh looked at him in amazement.

'You're the one whose natural instinct was to drive at a threatening buffalo,' observed Sally acidly. 'But you're right, we'll settle this once and for all,' she added, tucking a sheet round the unconscious form on the bed. 'You and I will stay.' Ignoring the protests of both men, she briskly suggested that they move the injured man to the car, resolutely refusing to meet Josh's imploring eyes as he and Paul complied.

Once Jonathan Wincombe was comfortably installed in the back seat of the Mercedes, Paul took Josh aside, speaking to him for several minutes. Though she strained her ears, Sally could hear nothing of what passed between them, then she saw the guide nod as Paul jotted something on a piece of paper and handed it to him.

It was while the two men were shaking hands that she noticed the sudden stiffening of Josh's body, and there was an anxious frown on his brow as he surreptitiously motioned her to join him by the car.

'Sally, I can't go,' he muttered defeatedly. 'I've just seen that bite on Morrant's neck...it's from a spider and quite a nasty one.' Sally froze, unable to speak. 'The worst that can happen to him is forty-eight hours of high fever—you'd be as good as on your own here if that does happen.'

'And the best?' she asked quietly.

'He could have no reaction at all—but it's a risk I'm not prepared to take.'

'Josh, you haven't any choice—your career's at stake.' As she spoke, she opened the car door and gave him a gentle shove. 'He'll be OK. He was a bit off-colour this morning, but he seems to be over it now.'

With a sigh of resignation, Josh climbed into the car. 'There's a bottle of aspirins in the first-aid kit; give him a couple—just to be on the safe side—they'd lessen any fever he might develop.'

Sally nodded and closed the door. 'Once you're out of the park you should reach the hospital in Chipata in next to no time in this—off you go.'

'Don't forget to boil any water you use,' fussed Josh as he started up the car. 'Even if it's for washing. I've kept a fire going in the cooking area and there's plenty of charcoal.'

Sally gave a sigh of exasperation. 'I shan't forget—now, off you go, Josh.'

'There are a few provisions we brought with us...'

'Josh!' she exclaimed. 'Both you and Wincombe are in urgent need of medical attention!'

'I'm going,' he promised, with a shadow of a smile. 'But get some aspirins into him...just in case. And for heaven's sake don't tell him what's bitten him—most Europeans die of fright when they learn they've been bitten by a spider.'

Sally watched as the large car disappeared from the clearing and was lost from sight in the undergrowth.

She was right to let Josh go—his livelihood was at stake, she told herself resolutely. And Paul Morrant was one of the fittest men she had come across...

'I was beginning to wonder if he'd ever go.'

The voice that interrupted her thoughts was so unfamiliarly absent-minded that Sally spun in alarm to find out why. Josh's information about the spider bite had frightened her more than she had been prepared to admit, she realised as she went weak with relief—his preoccupation was caused, not by his imminent collapse, but by the instructions on the can of sealant in his hand.

'As he said, twelve hours is the minimum this wretched stuff takes to do the trick. Couldn't you have picked something that works faster?'

Sally ignored the almost blatant provocation in his tone as she anxiously examined his face.

'I suppose I'd best do the necessary,' he muttered with a shrug, picking up the second can and dawdling his way towards the Land Rover.

He was definitely moving sluggishly, thought Sally as alarm began running riot in her mind. And she was certain that that peculiar lethargy had crept back into his voice.

'There's no need for you to do it now,' she pointed out, following him. 'Twelve hours from now will be midnight, and there's no way we can start off till daylight tomorrow! She made a conscious effort to tone the anxiety from her voice. 'It's mad to try doing anything now...it's the hottest part of the day.'

'The longer it's left in the radiator, the better,' he informed her and began unscrewing the cap.

Sally hovered uncertainly as he raised the bonnet.

'Strange as it may seem, I don't need supervision,' he announced irritably, scowling at her across the engine. 'Or perhaps you'd like to do it?'

Stung by the surliness of his tone, she turned on her heel and made her way back to the *rondavel*.

She was acting irrationally again, she told herself crossly—there were few spiders with a bite poisonous enough to kill a grown man, and none of those was indigenous to Zambia. She replaced the sheet on the bed Jonathan Wincombe had used, then checked the provisions Josh had mentioned.

When Paul eventually joined her in the cooking area to the back of the *rondavel*, she had boiled more water from the giant rainwater drum and was toasting the remainder of Aggie's sandwiches over the charcoal fire.

'Tea or coffee?' she asked as he slumped wearily to the ground. 'They're both black, I'm afraid.' She resolutely stifled a spontaneous stab of alarm at the sight of his exhaustion.

'Tea—Sally, I didn't mean to snap earlier... this heat doesn't seem to be agreeing with me.'

Sally's heart skipped a couple of unsettling beats. 'You know me—I never take offence,' she murmured, forcing humour into her tone. As she spoke she wondered if she should risk slipping a couple of aspirins into his tea. 'We'd best go inside and stay there—it'll be a lot cooler,' she advised and forced herself to look at him objectively. Yes, he did look limp and exhausted, she told herself firmly, but no more than she probably did—than anyone would in this appalling heat.

They could eat first, then she would tell him, she decided as he rose to his feet in silence.

Moments later, she was facing him across the small trestle table and watching with concern as he picked uninterestedly at a sandwich in front of him.

'I'm sure you'd feel a lot better if you ate something,' she suggested hopefully.

To her surprise, he picked up the sandwich, took a bite and began chewing mechanically. He brought it to his mouth a second time, then returned it to the plate.

'I'm sorry, Sally,' he muttered, and began rubbing his neck. 'You've gone to so much trouble...'

'Paul, it's OK,' she told him gently. She hesitated. 'It could be that bite on your neck...Josh saw it and warned me there was a possibility of your having a reaction to it.'

'Did he say what caused it?' His tone indicated no more than polite interest.

'A spider,' she answered evenly. She looked across at him to gauge his reaction, and frowned. His eyes seemed to be gazing into space, slightly to the left of her, while his hand rubbed mechanically at his neck.

'I can't say how grateful I am for the meal you have just provided, it was truly delicious.' His eyes suddenly focused on her and he smiled, oblivious of her expression of unconcealed anxiety, and then he began unbuttoning his shirt.

She leapt to her feet. 'I'll get you a couple of aspirins and then perhaps you should have a lie down,' she told him and went to the first-aid box. 'You'll feel better after a sleep,' she coaxed, handing him a glass of boiled water in which two tablets were dissolving, while struggling to suppress her growing certainty that sleep would have little effect on his increasingly strange behaviour.

He nodded co-operatively, drained the glass, then shook himself free of his shirt—fully exposing the angry rash on his neck. Gently, Sally drew her fingers across the tightly clustered trail of marks, then felt his brow.

It was hot, she told herself, but no hotter than would be expected in such heat.

Paul then proceeded to unzip his trousers and, with no trace of self-consciousness, stepped out of them.

Clad only in a pair of boxer shorts, he sat himself on the edge of one of the beds and watched as she picked up his discarded clothes and began folding them.

'I'm sure you'll feel better soon,' she murmured, conscious that she was offering comfort to herself as much as to him.

'Have you charmed fate too, Sally?' he suddenly demanded out of the blue, his tone truculent. 'Because it certainly seems to be on your side...stepping in and addling my brain at a time I needed it particularly clear.'

'Lie down, and try to sleep,' she urged softly, her concern turning to a gnawing fear at the rambling nature of his speech.

'Ah, sleep,' he muttered, with a humourless chuckle. 'Is sleep on your side too, Sally? It came to protect you from my questions last night...and now it seems it's to come and protect you from them once again. I don't want to sleep!' he exclaimed loudly, his voice angry.

He lurched unsteadily to his feet, then immediately fell back on the bed as his legs refused to support him.

'Please, Paul,' she begged, reaching out a hand that was angrily brushed aside. 'Don't fight it. You'll only feel worse.'

'What mustn't I fight?' he demanded wearily, stretching out on the bed and gazing sightlessly up towards the thatched roofing. 'The fact that I desire you? Or the fact that I cannot trust you? Because I can't trust you, can I, Sally?' His eyes turned to meet hers, and now there was no glazing to mist the sharp penetration of their scrutiny.

'Why do you say that?' she whispered, her voice a hoarse rasp of guilt.

'Don't answer my questions with rhetorical ones of your own,' he snapped. 'Does Josh Banda work for your company?'

'No,' she retorted, unsure why she should feel and sound as if she were lying. The fact that Josh had terminated his contract scant days ago was immaterial.

Unsettled and apprehensive, she seated herself on the edge of the second bed as he rolled over on to his stomach, pillowing his head on his arms.

'You don't deny I can't trust you. I find that most puzzling . . . in fact, I find you most puzzling, Sally.' His words were soft with the incipience of sleep. 'Puzzling, and quite inordinately desirable.'

Sally clenched her hands tightly in her lap as the breathless sigh of his words washed over her. There was a perverse need deep within her that seemed to welcome his statement that he found her desirable, but an even stronger need to be honest with him was tearing her apart.

'Paul, if I could, I'd be completely honest with you. But circumstances make it impossible . . . I've given my word . . . I have no right to risk all that could be at stake.' Even as the words tumbled from her she felt guilt—but a guilt far weaker than her desperate need for this token explanation. 'Paul, could you try to trust me?'

She waited in trepidation for his reply—panic rising in her at the realisation of the unforgivable weakness in which she had indulged, the consequences of which were unthinkable. Her eyes rose in dread to meet his, then widened in a mixture of relief and alarm. Paul Morrant was fast asleep.

Filled with restless confusion, Sally rose to her feet and went to where he lay. The dark profusion of lashes that fanned out against his cheeks were motionless and the mouth, full and sensuous, yet almost gentle in sleep, was parted slightly. For several moments she stood there, listening to the almost soundless sigh of his breathing.

More confused than ever, she moved away, pouring water into a shallow enamel pan before stripping off and sponging herself down. It was his stated lack of trust that had so unsettled her, she fretted as she donned a loose T-shirt and a pair of briefs. A mistrust that seemed to stem from the phone calls of the night before. With a groan of frustration she flung herself on the second bed—she could hardly ask to whom he had spoken and what had been said—all she could do was wait in dread for the next round of cross-examination and hope she survived it. She was just not cut out for this sort of subterfuge.

She shook her head as she gazed across at the lithe brown body on the next bed, so peaceful in sleep.

It had seemed so easy to promise silence to Lena—easy before she became embroiled in all it entailed. And now the thought of Paul regarding her as dishonest was one she found more and more disturbing.

Despite the airless heat that hung like an enervating weight in the darkened room, she gave a small shiver.

She should try a little honesty with herself. Face the fact that much of her trouble stemmed from the powerful attraction she felt towards a man she had only known a matter of days. Face her bitter resentment that fate was denying her the opportunity to find where this attraction, which she knew was mutual, might lead.

She was just beginning to doze off when the maddening whine of a mosquito brought her to instant frustrated awareness. She glared up accusingly at the thatching then, cursing savagely under her breath, rose and shoved her bed against Paul's. After letting down the single net hanging above them and tucking it securely around both beds, she climbed in—vowing that one word of innuendo from him, when he awoke, would definitely be his last.

But it was Sally who woke, several hours later, disturbed by the heavy, burning weight against her midriff. Drugged with sleep, she attempted to ease the weight from her and felt her hand cushioned on a tousled mass of damp hair.

Her eyes struggled to focus in the dim light. Paul Morrant was lying curled almost into a foetal position, his head wedged just below her ribs.

She slipped her hands to his shoulders to heave him aside, then froze with a gasp of shock at the terrible heat emanating from his body. Though drenched in perspiration, it was as though his skin were on fire.

In complete panic, Sally used her own body as a lever and rolled him over.

'Paul! Oh, my God, he's unconscious!' she cried, grabbing him by the shoulders and trying to shake him to awareness. 'Paul!'

'Get off me, will you?' he complained hoarsely. 'And stop shrieking at me, I'm not deaf.'

'Oh, thank God!' Weak with relief, she patted his cheek, only to have her hand irritably slapped aside.

'Go away,' he groaned and turned away from her on to his side. Ignoring his muttered protests, she felt his head—it burned like the rest of him.

Furiously chanting to herself to stop behaving like a panic-stricken moron, she dissolved three aspirins in water.

'Paul, drink this,' she pleaded, lowering the glass to his lips.

'Leave me alone.'

Like a large, mutinous child, he resisted her every attempt to raise his head, and kept his teeth clamped shut each time she brought the glass to his lips.

Drenched from her exertions, she eventually sank on the edge of the bed and stared disconsolately into the drink. Finally she deposited the glass on the table, then took a bowl and filled it with some of the water from her supply.

'This should make you feel a little cooler,' she told the inert form softly.

Dipping her flannel in the water, she sponged him gently from the back of his neck right down to his feet, and then down his arms, lightly towelling him dry as she went.

'Oh, for a crane to heave you over,' she sighed. Having found it impossible to move his head when he had resisted, there was no way she would be able to turn him.

She horrified herself by giving a shriek of alarm when he muttered incoherently and rolled on to his back.

'Paul, did you say something?' she croaked hopefully.

The enviably long lashes fluttered, then those cool blue eyes were gazing directly into hers. 'I said—all you have to do is ask. A crane won't be necessary.'

His voice was disconcertingly clear.

'What a relief,' managed Sally, slightly unnerved by the clarity of tone and even more so by the undisguised suspicion in his gaze. 'You know, I'm not trying to take unfair advantage of you.' What she had intended as a teasing reference to his remark of the night before sounded uncomfortably like a breathless protest to her ears.

'Sally, I hate to have to say this, but the way I feel at the moment you wouldn't get very far,' he murmured hoarsely, and those coolly implacable eyes remained on her as the colour leapt to her cheeks.

'I was trying to cool you off a little—in the hope it would wake you sufficiently to take these aspirin,' she informed him stiffly, suddenly hating him and dreading the cross-examination to come. He smiled wanly, then lifted himself on to his elbows and drained the glass she offered him. Then he immediately slumped back, totally exhausted.

'Sally, I'm sorry to be putting you to all this trouble,' he sighed, his eyes closed once more.

'It hasn't been any trouble,' she protested, overcome by remorse for that inexplicable flash of hatred.

He looked, and no doubt felt, ghastly, she thought guiltily, unsure whether she should finish sponging him down. The heavy sheen of perspiration gleaming on his body was all the answer she needed, though he neither moved nor even opened his eyes as she resumed her task, gently bathing his face, then his arms and upper body.

It was when she wrung out the flannel and placed it against a brown, tautly muscled thigh that he reacted, reaching out and grasping her wrist.

'Perhaps that wouldn't be the wisest of moves,' he told her softly. 'Even in my condition.' His eyes opened and he gave a low chuckle as he saw her obvious consternation. Then he raised her imprisoned hand to his burning lips and kissed it. 'If you could just learn to stop hurling optical daggers in your moments of inexplicable pique, you'd be the perfect nurse.' His breath was a hot caress against her palm, and Sally had to force herself not to snatch her hand away to escape the tingling awareness creeping up her arm and invading her body.

As she stood there, she became inordinately conscious of the fact that one long, muscular leg was lying sprawled across the bed that was hers; that the two beds were now technically one—one which, to all intents and purposes, she would be sharing tonight with a man who had only to kiss her hand to send her senses reeling.

'I'm sure you'll be the first to admit, though, that I make the model patient.' The grin that accompanied his words was positively angelic, though Sally took advantage of his slackening grip on her hand to remove it, in an attempt to bring some rationality to her wandering thoughts. There was nothing for them to be joking about, she reminded herself sharply. There had been no questions this time . . . but the time would come.

CHAPTER SEVEN

THE terrible threshing of his body began less than an hour after Sally had fallen into a troubled sleep.

In the end, bruised and in fear of having her legs broken by the restless flailing of Paul's, she staggered from the bed and lit a candle. Almost comatose from lack of sleep, she rescued the netting from around him and once more tucked it in. Then, with a safety-consciousness that came automatically to one raised in a dry, tropical climate she took the candle and stood it in a dish of water. The light would let her see what havoc he wrought to their cocoon and enable her to right it immediately. And, should the candle topple, at least there would be no danger of fire.

Wearily she dragged herself back into the tented shroud and, almost as though sensing her return, the sleeping man rolled towards her, imprisoning her with the arm he threw across her shoulders and the leg that curved over hers.

'Paul, you're throttling me,' she pleaded, and tugged his arm down a fraction.

Stifled by the heat and weight of him, Sally tried to free herself. It was when his hand reached up and entwined itself in her hair that she knew she was going to have to suffer in silence—each time she moved to free herself, he tugged painfully on her hair. Cautiously, so as to incur the minimum of retribution from those tugging fingers, she freed her trapped hand and with a sigh brought it to rest in the damp thickness of his hair.

As he had at other inopportune moments, he was now sleeping like a baby.

'Even when you're asleep you manage to be the most awkward individual I've ever come across,' she murmured softly, while her fingers played lazily in his hair.

Strange thoughts were churning in her mind as sleep came to claim her. The door of the *rondavel* seemed to drift open and the room became filled with daylight.

Lena and Eddie walked in: it was so good to see Eddie looking fit and well, she thought happily. Then Aggie arrived, followed by Mark and the two receptionists from Morrant-Gervaise-Morrant.

'I thought this was supposed to be a business trip,' accused one of the receptionists coldly.

Sally felt Paul stir against her.

'Of course it's a business trip...I should have thought that was perfectly obvious,' he growled.

It was Aggie's raucous laughter that started Sally off, and she was forced to bury her head in Paul's hair to stifle her giggles.

A sharp tug on her hair brought her back to reality.

'I can't sleep with you cackling right by my ear,' complained a hoarse, sleepy voice. 'What's so excruciatingly funny?' he demanded, raising his head and glowering in bewilderment at her. His look was one of such complete puzzlement that Sally felt convinced he had no idea who she was—the thought struck her as hilarious.

'Sally!' he growled warningly and yanked once more on her hair. She saw sluggish awareness enter his eyes as he extricated his hand and drew his body away from hers.

'I'm sorry...I...' he muttered, perplexed, and shook his head as though to clear it. 'Sally, what's wrong with me?' he asked quietly, an edge of uncertainty in his voice. 'Do spider bites always have this effect?'

She struggled upright, his tone triggering in her a desperate need to reassure him.

'I don't know,' she told him gently. 'But Josh said the worst it could be was a couple of days' high fever.'

'Let's hope he's right,' he muttered wearily, his hand automatically going to his neck.

'Paul, I'm sorry—really I am. Do you feel very bad?'

'Never felt worse,' he informed her laconically.

'The longest it can last is another day.'

'How comforting to know,' he drawled, flopping back exhaustedly. 'Now that I'm having one of my bouts of lucidity, how about your telling me a story to keep me amused?'

Sally stiffened. It had been inevitable that he should return to questioning her, yet his words had hit her like a bolt from the blue.

'It had better be a good story. My mother writes books for children, so I'm used to only the best.' Sally desperately wanted to look at his face—to see if it reflected the absence of sarcasm in his tone—but she didn't dare.

'Were you an only child?' she asked, suddenly intrigued.

He nodded. 'I was blessed with what would probably be described as an idyllic childhood...I had a pretty special father, too.'

'Had?' she asked, as he lapsed into silence.

'He died almost eight years ago—saving a couple of kids from drowning.' The terseness of his response brooked no further questions; it spoke of a loss that still brought pain. 'And you, Sally?' he asked. 'You speak of your father, but never of your mother.'

She shrugged. 'I hardly know her. She and Dad split up when I was just a toddler...she remarried and lives in Brazil, so there never was much in the way of physical contact.'

'God, how awful!'

'Not really,' she said. 'My parents discussed it very carefully before reaching the conclusion they did. They both knew I'd be better off with Dad...I've not exactly grown up to be a raving psychopath, and I'm really rather grateful to my mother for having had the guts to make such a decision.'

She watched in amusement as he tried to accept what he obviously found unpalatable.

'What age were you when you and your father came here?'

'Ten.'

'I suppose Lena's mother acted as a surrogate mother to you?'

She smiled as she shook her head. 'Actually, Aggie's the nearest to a mother either of us had. Lena's mother died giving birth to her and, like Dad, Jonas never remarried...not that Aggie ever gave up on her matchmaking attempts,' she chuckled.

'Poor old Aggie, she doesn't have much success. You really should put her out of her misery, you know; she can't wait to get you hitched.'

'I'm sorry if Aggie gave you the third degree,' she murmured.

'I'd gladly swop an hour of Aggie's third degree for even a one-minute respite from this headache,' he muttered, his face suddenly contorting with pain.

'Those aspirins should start working soon,' she whispered, feeling utterly useless as he raised his hands to his temples and clamped them against his head. 'Would it help if I massaged your head?'

She leaned over him, dread filling her as she watched him silently begin turning his head from side to side, his eyes screwed tightly shut as though trying to blot out the pain. She placed her fingers gently against his temples and with light, circular movements tried to assuage his agony. Much later, when his breathing had slipped into the peaceful rhythm of sleep and her fingers could function no more, she placed both her arms around him and allowed her head to rest against the cushion of his hair. She was acutely conscious of her every movement and of the strength of the need within her to hold him as she now did. And the terrible lethargy that seeped through her, she knew, had no bearing on her need for sleep. She had been drained by a fear more terrible than anything she had ever experienced before.

She had seen agony on this man's face and it had become her own, filling her with a mind-numbing fear with its intensity. Was there any name, other than love, for the feelings she was experiencing? She gave a small sigh of hopelessness as she looked down at the man in her arms—arms that were holding him in what could only be described as an embrace.

But what were arms for, she asked herself with another, deeper, sigh, if not to embrace a loved one?

'Why the sighs, Nightingale?' murmured a drowsy voice against her. 'I know you're not asleep,' it persisted, as she maintained a shocked silence. 'You make an exceedingly exhausting bedmate, you know. One minute you're giggling down my ear and the next you're heaving dirty great sighs down it. Not in the least conducive to a good night's rest.'

Neither had moved. 'How's the head?' she asked tentatively.

'You have magic hands, Nightingale. But tell me,' he continued, 'leaving aside the sighs for the moment, what brought on that earlier bout of giggling?'

Because the sigh was something she had no intention of discussing with him, she found herself quite happily relating the dream to him, realising, when it was far too late, that her words must inevitably draw his attention to the uncommon intimacy of their position.

She felt the laughter begin to rumble through him, then he froze and let out a groan. 'My head's not up to raucous laughter yet, I'm afraid,' he gasped, and her fingers returned automatically to his head.

'Is that helping?' she whispered after a while.

'Mmm...this one's only a tiddler compared to the one before.'

'Would you like more aspirin?'

He shook his head, then cursed softly with the pain it brought. 'Sally?'

'Paul.'

'Who's Mark? The one who came into your dream with Aggie.'

It surprised her that she had actually mentioned Mark by name.

'Someone I once thought I loved.'

'Ah, so Sally isn't in love after all,' he murmured.

'Just because I'm not in love with Mark doesn't mean to say I couldn't be with someone else,' she retorted crossly.

'You sound as though you fall in and out of love with remarkable ease,' he remarked blandly.

'No, I don't...I...anyway, what about you?' she demanded.

'I suppose this Mark character is the shrinking violet type,' he murmured complacently, ignoring her question completely and painting a vivid verbal picture of someone with all the appeal of a limp lettuce leaf.

'Oh, definitely,' choked Sally, laughing despite herself.

This time it caused her little surprise when, seconds later, she realised he was once more asleep. She was growing accustomed to the pattern taken by his bouts of fever... just as she was growing accustomed to the probability that there was no name, other than love, for her feelings towards this infuriating, bemusing and devastatingly appealing man, who had woken in her arms and later returned to sleep in them... without registering so much as a flicker of surprise.

CHAPTER EIGHT

THE rains came shortly after dawn.

At the first peal of thunder rending the air, Sally merely muttered a sleepy protest and buried her face deeper into the silky cushion of Paul's hair.

The second came as a series of ear-splitting whip-cracks, so close that the hissing explosion of lightning it preceded was no more than a heartbeat away. The air filled with the cool aroma of eucalyptus as the rampaging din of the heavens was muffled by the leaden patter of raindrops.

'Paul! Wake up, the rains are here!' she cried out in excitement, as those first drops swelled and thundered into an impenetrable, slicing sheet. 'Hear it, smell it! Isn't it magnificent?'

The head that rose from her shoulder was no more than a dim outline as dawn struggled to filter through the darkness of the storm. 'What's so bloody magnificent about it?' he growled morosely. 'The racket is deafening.'

The eyes that peered down at her, in that moment before he rolled away, were those of a stranger, and they sent a shiver of desolation through her.

With waking had come an almost fatalistic acceptance of loving him—as though it were so much a part of her that it no longer merited questioning. It was love that had brought her spontaneous need to share her joy with him—the magical, exhilarating joy she had first experienced as a child and never lost—the rains. Her heart was heavy as she slipped from under the netting and made her way out of the *rondavel*—the joy was gone.

By the time she had covered the short distance to the sheltered cooking area she was soaked to the skin, but she was unaware of it. Mechanically she started the fire and put water on to boil, while silently chiding the child within her for trying to recapture that exhilarating urge on awakening—to dance in primitive welcome under those first falling raindrops.

Shrugging the memory aside, and uncaring of her sodden clothing and hair, she fetched the water canister from the Land Rover and filled the radiator. Then she returned to the *rondavel* and began setting the small table.

'Which would you prefer, tea or coffee?' she asked woodenly in the direction of the bed.

'Tea.'

She heard him throw aside the netting. 'Sally...'

'Could you manage a whole tin of beans?' she interrupted tonelessly, reaching for the opener.

'I don't want any food. Sally...'

'You'll have to eat something.' Her voice remained lifeless.

'OK, I'll have some beans—but not a whole tin.' There was a distinctly uncomfortable edge to his tone.

Saying no more, Sally picked up a tin and left.

He was embarrassed, she told herself grimly as she savagely prodded the fire, and incapable of hiding the fact, moreover. And no wonder—with her mooning around like a lovesick adolescent. All she was suffering from was a massive dose of infatuation, she told herself, a long-drawn-out sigh escaping her as she half-heartedly stirred the beans. She rubbed her face wearily, wishing her thoughts had not seemed so much like a futile prayer...her complete exhaustion was making it impossible to think logically.

'Sally, please come back inside. You're soaked.'

She jumped, startled to hear his voice so close to her, then whipped round to face him and gave a gasp of horror. The pallor beneath his tan had given him an almost jaundiced appearance, and the darkness of beard lent a dishevelled look to his face.

'You're the one who should be inside,' she protested, as he leaned heavily against one of the upright poles. 'You look as though you're about to collapse.'

Taking a pan in each hand, she motioned him to follow her. 'Hurry,' she urged, as he stumbled into the *rondavel* behind her.

Inside, she placed both pans on the table. 'Dry yourself,' she ordered, flinging a towel in his direction. She made the tea, dished out the beans, then turned to tell him they were ready.

The towel still lay where it had fallen. Paul was seated on the edge of one of the beds, shivers racking his body as he gazed sightlessly into space.

With an exclamation of exasperation, she picked up the towel and dried his unresisting body, doggedly ignoring her inner panic. 'Shall I get you a T-shirt?' she offered.

He shook his head.

'The food's ready,' she told him, her voice softening as she saw the pain that lingered on his face.

He rose, shook his head dazedly, then went and seated himself at the table.

'May I have some aspirins, please?'

'When you've eaten,' she told him. 'They're better for your stomach after food.'

He lifted his gaze to hers and, as the haze seemed to drift from his eyes, both eyebrows rose in supercilious query. 'With your vast fund of medical knowledge, I'm amazed you didn't take up medicine,' he stated with biting sarcasm, before turning his half-hearted attention to his plate.

'I happen to like what I do,' she replied, her voice ominously quiet. 'And I don't possess that streak of masochism so vital in dealing with ingrates such as you.'

It was the look he gave her that snapped what was left of her control. She leapt to her feet and got the aspirin bottle. 'Here,' she snapped, slamming it down beside him. 'Do me a favour and take the lot!'

'Why don't you just sit down and eat?' he suggested, as though her outburst had never taken place, and, because she just did not have the energy to maintain it, the bulk of her anger subsided.

'How long is this likely to continue?' he asked conversationally, indicating the relentlessly falling rain.

'I've no idea,' she replied coldly.

'I suppose driving in it is out of the question,' he muttered, rearranging the barely touched beans with his fork.

'Unfortunately, you suppose correctly.' Though they almost choked her, Sally ate the beans.

Paul took a minute forkful, then pushed his plate aside.

'Sally...I'm not the ingrate I know I must seem.'

'You should eat,' she informed him tonelessly, ignoring his attempted appeasement. All she wanted was for the rain to stop and for them to be on their way—nothing else mattered, least of all anything he chose to say. She had had enough.

He pulled back his plate and eventually cleared it.

'Please may I have my reward now, Nightingale? My head's about to explode.'

She watched as he washed down the aspirins with the now cooling tea, giving a shake of his head and grimacing as he did so, and her anger was suddenly gone.

'Paul, I know how ghastly you must be feeling,' she told him gently. 'It's just that I'm so very tired and you . . . you have a way of expressing yourself that tends to irritate me.'

'How diplomatically put,' he murmured. 'Why don't you just tell me I'm a pain in the . . .'

'You took the words right out of my mouth,' she cut in scathingly, furious with herself for the weakness that had earned her nothing but rebuff. Angrily she picked up her plate and reached for his and found her wrist encircled by his hand.

'Sally, all this started out as an apology . . . where have the words I meant to say gone?' he asked hoarsely, shaking his head in an obvious effort to clear it.

'I don't know, Paul,' she sighed, replacing her plate and trying to release her imprisoned hand. 'I don't want to hear what you have to say . . . God knows, I'm trying to make allowances for the fact you're unwell, but you make it impossible at times.'

'Sally, can't you understand why I have to hurt you?' he whispered, the hand round her wrist drawing her to his side.

'Why?' she asked, her breath catching in her throat as she gazed down into the sleepy turbulence of his eyes.

He placed his hands on her hips, drawing her towards him till she was standing between his legs. 'Sally, you're soaking wet,' he murmured huskily, placing his cheek against her sodden midriff.

'Don't...Paul, please,' she begged, her eyes clouded with uncertainty as she gazed down at the black, tousled head against her. He would fall asleep soon, she kept telling herself, but the knowledge did nothing to halt the weakness that was melting through her.

'When you woke this morning, I felt you wanted to dance for joy in the rain. Was I right, Sally?' His head rubbed gently against her body.

'Yes!' The word was dragged from her like a protest as she fought a longing to put her arms around him.

'Wet and beautiful...like a mermaid,' he intoned against her. 'Are mermaids warm and passionate, or are they cold as ice?'

'Paul,' she whispered, taking his head in her hands and drawing him away from her, 'you must get some rest. When the rain stops, we'll need to be on our way,' she told him, her voice rendered breathless by the love she would be mad to deny and the unmistakable tenderness she was seeing in his face.

He nodded, but his hands began lifting the soaking T-shirt that clung to her body.

'No,' she whispered huskily, as she felt the rasp of his beard and the hot search of his mouth against her breasts. But she made no move to stop him as he drew the shirt up and over her head—all she did was lift her arms in compliance as he removed it completely.

It was the savage suddenness of the desire that flamed through her as his lips and hands began possessing her body that lent her the strength to tear herself free, and her breath was a hoarse rasp in her throat as she watched him sway uncertainly to his feet, then stagger precariously towards her.

'You can't walk away from my arms, Sally,' he mumbled indistinctly, leaning heavily against her as she began guiding him towards the bed. 'Not when I'm playing the game by your rules...I'm asking you no questions.' His voice was suddenly clear. 'That's what you wanted, isn't it, Sally? No questions.'

'Lie down, Paul,' she urged, unnerved by the drift of his rambling words, but even more panicked at the thought of him falling.

'Lie down, Paul,' he echoed savagely, collapsing on to the bed and dragging her with him. 'And lie down, Sally,' he murmured huskily, his lips searching against hers till her mouth opened to receive his.

Then she was lost in the restless, seeking urgency of his probing tongue as there awoke in her a hunger that threatened to obliterate all but its need for fulfilment.

Her body curved like a pliant flame to his, her breasts springing to taut life at the silken sensation of his skin on hers, then throbbing with a savage ache as his hands came between their bodies to cup them to him.

'No!' she cried out against the plunder of his lips. 'Paul...no.'

'Oh, Sally, don't you understand?' he whispered hoarsely. 'I couldn't ask you the questions I should any more than I could let you dance in the rain. Why is my punishment so much worse than any I ever meant to inflict on you?'

She felt the rasp of his beard against her skin as his lips trailed down to the hollow of her throat, but his strange words had brought her a merciful escape from the passion that had threatened to engulf her.

'Don't ask me those questions, Paul, just trust me,' she pleaded huskily, her hands gentle against his hair. 'Why do you speak of punishment?'

He lifted his head and gazed down at her. 'Because at this moment I want you more than I've wanted anything or anyone in my life before,' he told her tenderly, his smile filled with sweetness. 'And do you know what's going to happen, my darling temptress?'

She shook her head as he brought his face to rest next to hers, his words of endearment echoing through her mind.

'I'm going to fall asleep. My head is lurching in circles I'm fighting it so hard . . . but the irrevocable fact is that I'm going to fall asleep,' he informed her with the most rueful of smiles.

'Oh, Paul,' she whispered, her breath choking on laughter as her arms slid up round his neck. 'Is there time for you to tell me why you couldn't let me dance?' she asked softly.

'I've one of the keenest senses of self-preservation there is,' he murmured lazily, his eyes beginning to droop with sleep. 'How could I possibly have allowed you to dance in the rain when it might well have led to my loving you?'

'A fate worse than death?' she whispered huskily.

'A fate far worse than death.'

His eyelids fluttered shut.

'Paul . . .' she began, then knew her words could no longer reach him. For long moments her eyes drank in the dark, ravaged beauty of his sleeping face, then she drew his head down till his cheek was against her breast. And she held him very close to her, a tremulous smile hovering on her lips as she gently shook her head. Infatuation? Never—how could she have thought to fool herself? 'Why do I love you, Paul Morrant?' she asked the sleeping man in her arms. 'Is it because you're the most exciting individual I've ever met? Or because I had never truly known what it was to want a man physically till I wanted you? But that's only a powerful sexual chemistry... it wouldn't account for the ease with which you were able to steal my love.'

She gave a shiver as the strength of her terror in the face of his pain crept back into her mind, and her arms tightened round him in her attempts to dispel it.

'Perhaps it's because I've always had a weakness for the baddies,' she whispered against his hair. 'And by no stretch of the imagination could you ever be classed as a goodie.'

She heard his voice echoing in her mind as she drifted into sleep. Given time, Paul Morrant would come to love her... he had as good as admitted he was almost there.

'The rain has stopped and my head is no longer the venue for the Grand National.'

Sally opened her eyes to the man grinning down at her.

'I love you,' she murmured with a devastating simplicity and drew his head to hers.

'Out of the mouths of babes and sleeping mermaids,' he groaned softly in that moment before his mouth met, then began to feast on hers.

Where before his body had been drugged with its need for sleep, it was now taut with the sharpness of arousal, imparting its demands to her with an urgency that sent an answering need shuddering through her.

'My beautiful Sally, there can be no turning back this time,' he groaned against the mouth that murmured in incoherent intoxication against his. 'Sally, do you understand what I'm saying?' he demanded hoarsely, drawing back to gaze down at her through eyes almost navy in the darkness of their passion. 'Why are you so beautiful?' he breathed, the touch of his hands like the delicate wing of a butterfly as he traced the outline of her breasts. 'So beautiful,' he groaned, his breath a caress on her flesh as his head lowered towards her.

Then it was his tongue that replaced those sensitive, probing fingers, and she gave a soft moan of longing as her body arched in helpless need, drowning in the exquisite sensations of excitement that rippled through her with his every maddening touch. Her hands pulled him closer, exploring and caressing the muscled expanse of his back as though to imprint the memory of him for ever on them, while the sharp probe of his teeth on her flesh brought a sob of surrender to her lips.

Unable to contain what threatened to explode from within her, her head began turning from side to side in a restless, pleading urgency, her fingernails rasping in desperation against his back as her body swayed in an unconscious rhythm of invitation to his. There were so many words she needed to speak to him, words rendered an incoherent gasp by the ragged distortion of her breathing, words lost in the search of her lips against the moist warmth of his skin.

Then his hands grasped her shoulders, pinning her to stillness while his mouth returned in impassioned hunger to hers, bringing the wildness of excitement within her to a pitch that was almost an agony as his hands began a slow trail of exquisite torture down the length of her body.

His husky murmur of impatience as he discarded her only item of clothing became a soft, shuddering moan as her hands repeated what they had learned from his.

'Do you still say you love me?' groaned Paul, his face shadowy with desire as his naked, golden body hovered weightlessly over hers.

'I love you,' she whispered without hesitation, her arms drawing him to her.

And it was love that took charge of her body, releasing in her a wantonness hitherto unsuspected that exulted as the last vestiges of control left him and his body plundered hers, goaded to savage recklessness by the blatant message of hers.

Where he led, she followed, the wildness of his passion sparking a primitive abandon of response in her till an exquisite madness took them beyond all dimensions of ecstasy to a shivering explosion of fulfilment.

Sally was still striving to control the ragged disorder of her breathing when he rolled over, carrying her with him till she lay against the tumultuous rise and fall of his chest.

She felt the play of his hands in her hair and raised her face to look down at him. His eyes were still filled with the languorous aftermath of passion, but there was a disbelieving grin on his face as he shook his head slowly from side to side.

'What?' she demanded breathlessly, before her lips succumbed to the temptation of exploring that grin.

'You have a disconcertingly underdeveloped sense of danger, my rash Sally,' he murmured huskily.

'Explain,' she whispered, nibbling at the corner of his mouth. 'My mind's no longer functioning.'

Tugging on her hair, he drew her face away from his. 'Hell, what have I done to you?' he muttered, his fingers gently tracing the livid mark on her shoulder where his teeth had branded the marks of his passion. He frowned. 'It's crazy, but I had no idea...Sally, your first experience of lovemaking should have been so much more gentle...I could easily have hurt you, frightened you...'

'But you didn't,' she protested.

'But I could so easily have,' he repeated woodenly, then, with a sigh, he guided her head till it rested at the curve of his throat. 'Sally, if I fall asleep on you now it will be against all my better instincts. But it will have precious little to do with spider bites; that's just about over.' His hands faltered in their delicate tracing of her spine. 'I wonder how long it will take for me to recover from your bite, though.' There was no edge to his tone, yet those casually spoken words had a dousing effect on the joy that still seeped through Sally.

'Paul... why do you say that?' she asked, unable to stop herself, though part of her dreading what she might hear.

'Ask me another time, my sweet,' he murmured sleepily. 'Though I think you already know the answer.'

Sally lay numbed and silent in his arms while the movement of his hands gradually ceased altogether as sleep claimed him. But all wonderment and joy had left her, eroded by his words and the nagging insistence of newly forming doubts.

He had warned her—speaking of questions unasked because they were those she wished to avoid.

He had accepted her candid declaration of love—but had given her no words of love in return.

She tried to silence the panic thudding in her heart.

The Paul Morrant she had first met would have thought nothing of mentally bludgeoning her with any questions he might choose to ask. But now there was a tenderness in him that had held him back. And his questions could only concern her silent protection of Zambezi Safaris... hardly a crime to cause a man such as Paul Morrant to withhold his love.

He *was* close to loving her, she told herself, her need to boost her faltering confidence desperate. And she would ask him again why he had so foolishly compared her love to the bite of a spider... the strength of her love had the power to topple him over the brink on which he hovered, and she had every intention of using its power.

Gently, so as not to disturb him, she eased herself from his arms, and half an hour later the small camp site was stripped of their presence and everything returned to its proper place.

Inside, the *rondavel* was the same, and there was a dull sadness in Sally as she climbed on to a chair and folded the mosquito netting. Soon they would leave this small room that had become the centre of her entire world, and the uncertainty that hovered like a black storm cloud over her made her want to cling and hide herself away in its familiar sadness.

'What on earth are you doing?' Paul's voice was husky with sleep as he grinned up at her.

'Being the perfect housekeeper,' she retorted, her heart turning somersaults of love as she watched him lazily stretch his long, athletic body and sit up, the look he gave her banishing all doubts from her mind. 'We should get going—that gives us a good four hours to get out of the park before dark.'

She stripped and folded the sheets from the bed as he dressed.

'You have been busy,' he murmured, walking toward her.

Sally's breath became a sharp gasp as she saw the expression on his face.

He halted before reaching her.

'Perhaps it's best if I blow you a kiss when we're on our way,' he told her, his smile amused but his voice husky with regret. 'The consequences of kissing you now would wreak havoc with our timetable.' He reached out and gave her a gentle shove towards the door as the happiness exploding in her bubbled into laughter.

*   *   *

'Switch off the ignition,' he told her ten minutes later when the Land Rover had resisted all their attempts to start it. He lifted the bonnet and gave a groaning laugh. 'It's full of rainwater—I'll have to dry off what I can.'

'How long will it take?' asked Sally, climbing out and joining him. 'We can't cut it too fine.'

He shrugged. 'It's had a pretty thorough soaking. I'll see what I can do—you wait inside, it's sweltering out here.' Over an hour later, Sally heard the engine splutter to life, then die immediately and seconds later Paul appeared at the door, wiping his hands on a towel covered in grease.

'All we can do is leave the bonnet up and let the sun finish drying it off.'

'But we can't drive when it's dark,' she whispered.

'Oh, dear,' he mocked softly, then slipped the towel over her head and drew her towards him with it. He released the ends of the towel and cupped her face in his hands. For a moment his eyes were dark with need, then they suddenly widened in surprise and he burst out laughing.

'Oh, Sally, I'm sorry, I've covered you with grease.'

'I don't care!' she cried, flinging her arms round him and raising her mouth invitingly to his.

All it took was his touch, she thought in wonder as his arms slid around her and his mouth hungrily answered the invitation of hers, just his touch, and she was lost in the melting fire of her need for him.

'Darling,' he murmured against her lips. 'Are we going to have to go through the performance of lighting a fire and boiling water before we can wash?'

Sally froze in his arms, unable to believe she was hearing correctly. His expression was a mixture of teasing and passion as he gazed down into her startled eyes.

'We can hardly leave our oily imprints over those sheets you've so neatly folded and will now have to unfold, can we now?'

'I was so busy folding them I forgot to empty the pails of boiled water,' she informed him with a raggedly breathless laugh.

'So,' he murmured, rubbing the tip of his nose against hers. 'If you were to get the wash things, our problem could be solved.' Because his arms tightened unco-operatively around her when she made to do as he had suggested, it was several moments before she managed to get outside.

When she returned he had drawn the beds back together and replaced the sheets.

He gave her a low, mocking bow as her face registered amused disbelief.

'Mechanic, bedmaker and now . . .' He paused to draw her to him. ' . . . and now launderer *extraordinaire*,' he whispered. 'Don't move, you happen to be the laundry,' he warned, taking the washbag from her.

His eyes never once met hers as he gently removed the marks from her face and, though she was trembling visibly from the effect of his nearness, there was no expression, other than frowning concentration, on his handsome features.

'You'll have to remove your top if I'm to do this properly.' The huskiness in his voice belied the remoteness of his expression. She removed her T-shirt, then gasped with the shock of excitement that shuddered through her as his hands reached out for her breasts.

Even as he touched her, he drew his hands away and gave a hoarse, groaning chuckle. 'Seems I've just given myself more cleaning up to do,' he whispered, his eyes glittering pools of desire as they gazed down on the tautened mounds of her breasts, where streaks of oil from his hands now contrasted starkly with the cream of her flesh.

'Perhaps if you were to wash your hands, you'd make your task that bit easier.' She had difficulty getting out the words, so heavy was the suffocating thud of her heartbeat.

She took the flannel from him and carefully washed each of those hands with their strong, elegantly tapering fingers. Then she wiped away the traces of oil clinging to the hairs of his chest, though when her fingers then began trespassing in that silken blackness they were immediately removed.

'I haven't finished,' he admonished huskily, then slid open the zip of her slacks and drew them down over her hips. 'Now the pants,' he told her when she had stepped out of the slacks. When she was naked before him he began removing the smears of oil from her breasts, his light, impersonal touch teasing her to a hunger she found impossible to contain.

'No!' she begged, flinging her body against his, her arms clinging and dragging his head down to hers.

'Why were you so long stopping me?' he groaned as his lips crushed down on hers.

His hands began raking her body with a fevered impatience, then with a hoarse cry he shed his clothing and swept her up into his arms. The blackness of his hair became streaked with tawny strands of hers as he carried her to the bed, his lips searching hotly against the curve of her neck.

And again their lovemaking was a wild abandonment of all reason, a fearless ferocity of mutual need that soared and hovered till the shattering explosion of its culmination possessed them. In those long moments it took Sally to drift out of her realm of enchantment, a small smile played on her lips as she lay in perfect contentment with her cheeks against his chest...she no longer had any doubts.

'Dinner is served, m'lady.'

Sally opened her eyes to find the room bathed in candlelight.

'Paul, what time is it?' she gasped, sitting upright.

'Gone seven, and high time you stirred yourself.'

Bleary-eyed, she slipped into pants and a T-shirt, then went to the table. The inevitable beans lay steaming on two plates.

'You shouldn't have been out there in the dark!' she protested in horror.

He shrugged and grinned. 'I clattered around as noisily as I possibly could—I probably scared off everything within a ten-mile radius.' He passed her a steaming mug of coffee. 'I also got the Land Rover going, and I've taken the precaution of putting it under cover in case it rains again.'

She looked at him in amazement. 'You *have* been busy!' she chuckled, and tucked into the beans—she was starving.

'You notice how much more appetising the beans are when subjected to my culinary skills,' he murmured. 'I've also managed to provide a dessert.'

'Good God!' shrieked Sally. 'You've not been out picking fruit, have you? Paul?'

'Miss Hughes,' he drawled mockingly. 'I've no suicidal tendencies. I merely showed a bit of enterprise and opened those unlabelled tins.'

'And?' she demanded laughingly.

'We have peaches and rice pudding to follow...at least, I think it's rice pudding,' he added dubiously.

His doubts proved groundless, and as they later sat sipping their coffee Sally congratulated him on what she swore was the best meal she had had in months.

'Though I must say a cigar would round things off nicely,' she added wistfully.

'Be my guest, though I wasn't aware you were partial to them.'

'Not for me,' she protested as he produced the gold case and lighter. 'It's just that the smoke might ward off those wretched mosquitoes—can't you hear them?' she asked, swatting yet another aside.

She watched as he went through the ritual, studying the deft movements of those long, slim fingers and wondering whether she preferred him bearded, as he practically was now, or clean-shaven. His eyes flickered across to hers, then back to the cigar he was just about to light, and a shiver of coldness ran through her at the remoteness in that unguarded glance.

She had imagined it, she argued with herself as smoke drifted up around him, making confirmation impossible. They were lovers, she reminded herself with a small frisson of shock. Yet now they could be taken for acquaintances merely sharing a table...while moments before she had been so certain she was loved.

She wanted to reach out, as any normal lover might do, and place her hand in the security of his.

Instead, her eyes hovered on the hand that toyed idly with the gold lighter, strong, tanned and impersonal—yet it was a hand that had caressed her body to wild heights of passion.

The fingers stopped their idle play and her eyes rose to meet the cool questioning of his. It was a look so utterly impersonal that Sally's mouth was suddenly dry with fear.

'You . . . you're very brown.' Her words were random, a reflex reaction to spare her from examining her growing feelings of apprehension. 'Is it because you sail a lot?'

His eyebrows rose a fraction. 'How do you know I sail?'

'You told me . . . yesterday,' she murmured stiltedly, puzzled that he seemed to have no recollection of having done so.

'I race mostly, and usually muffled to my ears in oilskins. But I suppose my passion for the sea accounts for my permanent tan. Does that satisfy your curiosity?'

His tone had hardly been that of a lover exchanging small confidences, and Sally gave a small, hopeless shrug as she felt the colour rise on her cheeks.

'Sally, are you sure that was what you intended asking me?'

The abruptness of the question startled her, just as the coldness in his tone appalled her.

'Or perhaps you are no longer interested in why I should feel the need to recover from my interlude with you.'

His interlude! Sally felt herself physically recoil from the cold impersonality of those words. But the fact that he regarded what they had shared as a mere interlude was explanation enough as far as her shattered ego was concerned.

Numbed to silence, she was filled with what he had told her—without his even having to resort to words— he had taken what had been so blatantly offered to him.

He was an obviously virile man—so who could blame him? And who but a blindly romanticising fool would have hoped for love?

'You can't expect to be allowed to change the rules half-way through the game, Sally.' His words suddenly cut across the bleak wasteland of her thoughts. 'Especially when we were playing by your rules...no questions.'

A game, with rules—even though they were rules she had had no option but to set—that was all it had been to him. The truth, even had she been free to tell him, would have made no difference at all...it had only been a game...a brief interlude.

'Why quibble?' she retorted, pride toning the misery from her voice and substituting a harsh ring of coldness. 'It will all be over by tomorrow...no more rules...no more questions unasked and unanswered,' she continued, her words a challenge, while her foolish heart still begged for his denial.

For a moment, Paul's eyes blazed across the table at her, then he shrugged and rose to his feet. 'I'm afraid I'm about to crash out. If possible, I'd like to leave at dawn.'

Sally remained at the table, lost in the stunned emptiness of her thoughts as he let down the netting and threw himself on to one of the beds.

For several hours she sat there, while the emptiness became filled with bitterness and grief till eventually, exhausted not only from the battle that raged within her, but also from the maddening threat of mosquitoes, she slipped silently under the netting and heard the soft breath of his untroubled sleep.

Despite the intensity of his presence in her life, the time had been so short, she began telling herself as she lay tensely on her side as far from him as possible...and she would recover. Time would heal far more quickly than she could now believe possible—it had healed once before . . . but before there had been so little to heal. She buried her face against the pillow to stifle her hopelessness.

But sleep tricked her into forgetting her despair for a while, when it brought her the gentle comfort of his arms, and the gentleness remained in him when she clung to him in a silent plea to dispel her fears.

And it was there when their bodies met in a poignant tenderness of passion, so different from anything they had shared before. But his gentleness, in the end, brought her only increased despair as later she sobbed in hopeless exhaustion in his arms. Though the tenderness of his body had seemed to promise all she could ever ask, his silence was an implacable denial that there had ever been any promise.

CHAPTER NINE

'WOULD you mind pulling over here? I have some phone calls to make.'

Sally drew the Land Rover to a halt before the bottle store in Lundazi.

They had scarcely exchanged more than half a dozen words since they had left the game camp at dawn, and those had been in the carefully impersonal tones he had just used.

'Sally... I didn't want it to be like this.' Suddenly the remoteness was gone and there was desperation in his voice. 'I must have been out of my mind... behaving like an ostrich when I always knew the facts would have to be faced.'

'Does it really matter, Paul?' she asked wearily. What the hell did he expect—her apology for complicating his little interlude by falling in love with him? 'Go and make your calls.'

She was conscious of his hesitation before he stepped down from the Land Rover, but she refused to meet his eyes.

In the twenty minutes it took for him to reappear she deliberately blanked her mind, for a while examining the skies and trying to work out how long it would be before the gathering rainclouds spilled down on them. Then, when she had seen everything there was to be seen on the deserted street, she returned her attention to the clouds, examining each one until she could almost predict the coming shape of their ever-changing patterns. She

145

did everything in her power to prevent herself thinking.

'I'll drive.'

Slowly, she turned her blank gaze to Paul's face at the window.

'Sally, you'll have to let me take over at some point,' he informed her, his voice once again chillingly impersonal. She shrugged and moved over to the passenger seat. Desperate for something to occupy her mind, she had refused all his previous offers, but now her increasing feeling of exhaustion warned her it would be foolish, if not dangerous, not to comply.

'You even lied about Josh Banda,' he informed her tonelessly as he started up the engine. 'Did you honestly think I wouldn't find out he works for Zambezi Safaris?'

'He doesn't,' she replied hoarsely, her heart sinking. 'That was one lie I didn't have to tell you—I take it you've known the reason for my telling you the others for some time.' There seemed little point in trying to keep up the charade, she reasoned hopelessly.

She turned as she became conscious of his eyes boring into her, and it was all she could do not to flinch from their naked hostility. 'It's tantamount to sacrilege, isn't it, Paul, for anyone to lie to you or disrupt your precious peace of mind?' she rasped, her tone savage with hurt.

'If you want us to get to Chipata in one piece, I suggest you keep your mouth shut,' he hurled back at her, lurching the vehicle to greater speed as he slammed his foot hard on the accelerator. 'One thing's for sure—you deserve all that's coming to you!'

Sally gave a croaked travesty of a laugh. 'Whatever happens to me, there's one consolation—you won't be around to gloat.'

When he made no reply, she huddled in her seat, a part of her mind trying to blot out the naked loathing in the words that had passed between them, while another part stubbornly refused to accept what her ears had heard. By the time they drew to a halt beside the Mercedes in the forecourt of the Chipata hospital, not another word had passed between them.

She turned as he let out a long, shuddering sigh and dropped his head on to the hands still gripping the steering wheel. 'If the keys are in the Mercedes, I suggest you take it and go,' he told her with that same terrible tonelessness.

'You what?' she gasped, unable to believe her ears. If he had hit her the effect could have been no more destructive than those coldly dismissive words. She had not even been conscious of the rain starting, but it fell like a balm on her burning face as she flung herself out of the Land Rover.

'Sally, for God's sake don't be so bloody stupid!' he rasped, grabbing her by the arm as he reached her side.

'Let go of me,' she told him with quiet fury, wrenching free her arm.

'Why, Sally?' he begged hoarsely.

'Why?' she shrieked, her reason deserting her. 'Why? Why? Why? What are you, Paul—a sphinx? I don't understand you and your stupid, enigmatic riddles, and I don't want to! Go away and just leave me alone! Go back to your own small world where everything is cut and dried and there's no such thing as compromise!'

'For God's sake, Sally, I've been compromising all along...'

'Sarah Elizabeth Hughes?'

Sally spun round at the sound of those barked-out words. There were four men, two of them Europeans who, with one of the two Africans, stood in the shelter of the hospital porch. The fourth man, the uniformed

Zambian policeman who had spoken, stood in the rain by her side.

'I'm Sally Hughes,' she answered, her eyes flying to Paul, whose face was drained of colour.

'Miss Hughes, you are under arrest as an accessory to grand larceny.'

The policeman's words of caution were lost in the turmoil of Sally's mind.

Arrest...larceny...the words reverberated in her head.

'Is this someone's idea of a joke?' she demanded, her voice faltering. 'Paul...what's happening to me?'

Her choked words of disbelief cut across the tirade of abuse he was hurling in fluent French in the direction of the two Europeans. He spun round to face her, his eyes agonised, at the very moment she became conscious of the policeman placing handcuffs around her unresisting wrists.

'Get those bloody things off her!' Paul Morrant's voice was cracked with rage as he turned in fury on the obviously embarrassed policeman. 'I warned you, but you wouldn't listen...'

'You warned me?' she shrieked at him, suddenly struggling like one possessed to free herself. 'Is this what you meant when you said I deserved all that was coming to me?'

'Sally, stop struggling,' he begged.

'Is this what you meant, Paul...this?'

'I'll try to get it sorted out.' His voice was hoarse and ragged. 'But please, Sally, don't struggle.'

It was pride that halted her panic-stricken attempts to free herself, and pride alone that suddenly calmed her voice as she spoke. 'I've asked you twice, yet somehow you can't bring yourself to answer me, can you, Paul?'

She turned and looked up at her captor. 'Please take these off me . . . I've done nothing wrong.'

His expression decidedly uncomfortable, the policeman began guiding her gently out of the rain.

Sally heard Paul's voice, loud and angry, in the furious babble of French that broke out as she and the constable moved away—the voice of the man who had been unable to deny his responsibility for the terrible indignity to which she was being subjected. Even when the handcuffs were eventually removed from her, she made no attempt to wipe the rain from her face, and its traces lingered like tears on her cheeks when, what seemed like a lifetime later, she was led to an awaiting police car. It was as though something inside her had died.

The first thought that was in any way coherent came to her as a kindly, anxious-looking young policewoman led her into a cell—Chipata police station was an extraordinarily pretty place. Even beneath the dark gloom of stormclouds, it was a picture of whitewashed charm—almost like an old English cottage. And how could a prison cell look so bright, so clean—almost inviting?

A prison cell! She stopped in her tracks, bumping against the girl at her heels, a strangled cry of horror choking in her throat. 'What am I doing here?' she begged of the Zambian girl now beside her.

The policewoman placed a comforting arm around her. 'Miss Hughes, why don't you have a shower and change into some dry clothes? We have your bag here.'

Sally looked at the girl in total bewilderment.

'You'll feel a lot better then,' urged the soft Zambian voice. 'And after, we can talk.'

The policewoman maintained a discreet presence while Sally showered and washed her hair. She was even full of apologies for not being able to produce a hair dryer. When she smilingly offered to help towel dry the thick blonde hair, her kind words brought a sudden rush of tears to Sally's eyes and she turned away in embarrassment and buried her face in the towel.

'What in God's name am I doing here?' she begged brokenly.

'Miss Hughes...'

'My name's Sally!' she cried out. 'Please.' Her voice dropped to a hoarse whisper. 'Please...my name's Sally.'

'And I'm Mary—Mary Kashoki. Please, Sally, put these clothes on, then we can talk.'

A portly constable brought in a tea tray just as they re-entered the cell, and when the man muttered a few words to Mary in Bemba the policewoman shook her head, which brought an immediate smile of satisfaction to his face.

'It seems Constable Langa didn't like the idea of locking the door; I've told him it won't be necessary,' murmured the Zambian girl with a conspiratorial smile. Sally managed a wan smile in reciprocation. Whatever the reasons for her being here, she was being shown nothing but kindness.

'I take it Mr Morrant felt it advisable not to say anything to you.'

'What could he possibly say to justify this?' blurted out Sally.

Pity and puzzlement flickered quickly across the girl's face before she managed to control it. 'I'm an Inspector with Special Branch,' she began, motioning Sally to be seated and pouring them both some tea. 'About two weeks ago we were contacted by Interpol regarding a possible computer fraud being perpetrated by a foreign national in this country.'

As the girl spoke, Sally found her mind being distracted by trivial observations, such as the way the leaf pattern on her cup was just a shade lighter than that of the one Mary drank from.

'Sally, are you hearing me?' asked the Zambian girl sharply, her eyes troubled.

Sally nodded. 'He wanted the codes from Jonathan Wincombe,' she muttered disjointedly, her mind refusing to accept what she was being told. 'How can you steal from a computer? I don't understand any of this.' Her words were like a plea.

'With the right codes it's all too easy to transfer money via a computer,' stated Mary quietly. 'And you have been arrested because a million pounds sterling was paid into the account of Zambezi Safaris.' Her eyes met Sally's. 'We have reason to believe that money was part of a three-million-pound theft from Morrant-Gervaise-Morrant.'

'No!' protested Sally weakly. 'No...this isn't happening. I can't believe this can be happening!'

'Drink this, you'll feel better.'

Sally accepted the cup being pressed into her hand and gazed at it sightlessly. Suddenly she was giggling helplessly, then stopped abruptly as she felt the sting of hot tea against her hand. 'But surely our bank explained...' Her words petered to silence as the terrible realisation that logic could no longer be applied to her life began to dawn on her.

'Your bank can explain the money?' probed Mary Kashoki.

'Obviously not,' snapped Sally, desperation flooding through her. 'I'm under arrest.' Courtesy of the man she loved, who regarded her as no more than a thief.

'A warrant was issued to search your Lusaka offices on Thursday and bank statements were studied. We are interviewing your bank manager tomorrow, Monday.'

'Why didn't you speak to him on Friday?' asked Sally wearily. 'It would have spared me all this,' she added, spreading her hands in a gesture of hopelessness.

Mary Kashoki reached out and laid a hand on her arm. 'Friday, unfortunately, was a Bank Holiday.'

'What about Jonathan Wincombe? What about Mark Shelby?' demanded Sally frantically.

'Wincombe hasn't been questioned yet, he only came off the danger list last night. And Shelby has disappeared.'

Sally gave a shrug of defeat, drained her cup and then replaced it. A small, hard smile was playing on her lips. She had nearly gone out of her mind worrying about the possibility of Zambezi Safaris being linked with hunting...while all along Paul Morrant had her branded in his mind as an out and out criminal. Paul...

She had to wipe all thought of him from her mind.

'What happens between now and Monday... tomorrow?' The words came out in a rush.

'As soon as you're ready, a driver will take us to Lusaka.'

'And?'

'The full charges will be read out to you when we get there.'

'Full charges?' gasped Sally. 'Don't tell me there's more! Mary, I'm sorry,' she apologised suddenly. 'You've been kindness itself. But how can I be under arrest? My bank hasn't even been consulted...'

'They have other evidence...Sally, if I knew what it was, I wouldn't be at liberty to say.'

Mercifully, she slept for the entire journey to Lusaka, and when she stepped out of the car at the capital's main police station she accepted the terrible exhaustion that still gripped her as shock. But it was the sight of the familiar faces of Aggie and Alphonse, now tense and drawn with anxious love, that was her undoing. She felt Alphonse's hand, heavy in its symbolic protection, on her back as she flung herself into Aggie's arms.

'Oh, my poor child, what are they doing to you?' choked Aggie, hugging her tightly.

'They're being very kind to me...oh, Aggie, why am I here?' she sobbed, unable to hold back her pent-up misery.

'*Bwana* Paul will sort it out,' soothed Aggie confidently. 'He's here...and he'll sort it out.'

The words only served to increase Sally's sobbing, but there was no way she could bring herself to disillusion Aggie, and gradually she managed to pull herself together, gratefully accepting the snowy white handkerchief Alphonse thoughtfully slipped her. It was some time before she could persuade the couple to go back home and wait for her there.

'There's no point in your hanging around while I get this sorted out, my loves,' she pointed out, summoning up a smile.

'Anyway, *Bwana* Paul will see to it,' nodded Aggie; her faith was unshakeable.

Sally kept the travesty of a smile firmly in place as she nodded and waved them goodbye.

It was just as the desk sergeant had begun reading the charges against her that Paul Morrant emerged from a door to the back of the man. He was directly in her line of vision and all she had to do was raise her head for her gaze to be level with his. She lifted her head, and her pride rejoiced as she saw him flinch beneath the scorn and anger blazing from her eyes.

This was the man who had taken her love, taken her body, while in his mind he had branded her a thief. She had fallen in love with a man who had spun a web of laughter and tenderness around her—a deceit he had so skilfully used to conceal the coldness of his calculating heart.

As the pain and hatred within her poured itself out towards him, she gradually became aware of the silence around her. The charges had been read, yet she had heard not a single one of them. But they all, whatever they were, had stemmed from the man whose hoarse pronouncement of her name now broke the silence.

'Sally, I wanted all charges against you dropped...but I no longer have any say in the matter.'

'Why should you, of all people, want the charges against me dropped?' she asked, her voice a cold and brittle contrast to the hurt and anger that blazed within her.

'I want you out of here. I'm trying to arrange bail...Sally, believe me, I didn't mean it to be like this.'

'What exactly did you expect?' she asked with cold venom. 'And why the sudden change of heart, Paul? After all, it's turned out very well for you...you even had your little interlude thrown in for good measure—and all with no questions asked. I really can't see what you're complaining about.' She stiffened as her voice threatened to break, but she couldn't stem the flow of her bitter words. 'I realise now that the rules were all yours—and never mine. And as for your hypocritical offer of bail, forget it! I'd rather spend ten years in Siberia than take help from you!'

'Sally, you don't have to keep up the pretence any more . . . you'll need all the help you can get,' he told her wearily.

'If you're so hell-bent on making yourself useful, I suggest you go round to Aggie and Alphonse and break the good news to them—that thanks to you I'll be spending the night in jail.'

His eyes held hers and, as the seconds seemed to drag into hours, she never once flinched from that cold gaze. Then he was gone, his mouth a harsh line of fury in that moment before he turned his back on her and left.

With Mary Kashoki and another Zambian officer present, she was questioned by the two men she now knew were from Interpol. Both spoke good, though heavily accented English.

Several times, the two Zambian officers intervened on her behalf when she found it impossible to answer questions that meant nothing to her.

'We *have* no Swiss bank accounts. How many times do I have to tell you?' she demanded wearily. 'Just one in Guildford and one here in Lusaka, and anyone can tell you that our particular branch just happens to be the most incompetent there is. No doubt you'll find that out tomorrow for yourselves, just as you'll find out that money was never intended for Zambezi Safaris.'

'But Mark Shelby is an employee of Zambezi Safaris,' intoned the older, more hectoring of the two Europeans.

'He's not!' she groaned, having made the same point several times before. Through clenched teeth she went once more through Mark's extra-curricular activities at the expense of Zambezi Safaris. 'Why the hell don't you find him and ask him yourself?' she finished wearily.

'Find him?' demanded the man.

'Yes, find him,' she retorted angrily. 'A fat lot of good your surveillance did!'

'How did you know he was under police surveillance, Miss Hughes?' She wished she had kept her mouth shut, as there immediately followed a detailed and mind-numbing session of questioning on her meeting with Mark.

At first she held back, remembering Mark's words about his guard having done him a favour by letting them meet, then she realised she was in no position to be so charitable.

As the questions droned on, all sense of time deserted her and her head was still swimming from the barrage of words as she sat alone with Mary Kashoki what she felt must be several hours later.

'I'm beginning to understand how completely innocent people end up behind bars,' she conceded miserably, as she picked listlessly at the meal sent in to her. 'Even to my own ears I sounded as though I was telling a pack of lies...people just don't remember dates and times and all those details; why should they?'

'But you didn't sound much like an accomplished fraudster,' smiled the policewoman, then pulled a small face. 'I don't think I should have said that.'

Sally smiled weakly. 'That's another thing that worries me...the guard on Mark Shelby...'

'That's all right. We already knew of his involvement. It was he who later...lost Mr Shelby,' murmured Mary wryly.

'Why have you been assigned to me, Mary? You're a full Inspector, hardly a rank to be given guard duty.'

The girl smiled. 'I'm also a woman,' she laughed. 'And there aren't that many of us in Special Branch.' She hesitated, her eyes examining Sally closely. 'Perhaps this is another of those things I shouldn't be saying, but I'm sure you'll be freed tomorrow. Sally, you must try to forget where you are tonight...think happy thoughts and forget your surroundings.'

But she had no happy thoughts to blot out her surroundings. All she had was the inescapable fact that the man to whom she had given her love had not found it in his heart to give her a warning. Perhaps his conscience had pricked him into telling her to take the Mercedes and go...but even then there had been no word of warning.

His belief in her guilt had been absolute, as absolute as the love she had given him.

'Sally.' There was a smile of pleasure on Mary Kashoki's face as she entered the cell the following morning. 'I've come to take you home—you're free!' The smile died on the Zambian girl's lips as she saw the blank misery on the lovely face that turned to her. 'The bank manager confirmed every word you said—the poor man is almost suicidal over the trouble caused. And Mark Shelby walked in here about an hour ago.' She frowned as her words met with no response. 'My dear, it's all over.' The Inspector placed a hand on Sally's shoulder. 'Are you all right?'

Sally made a concentrated effort to respond. 'Yes...I'm all right,' she murmured. 'I suppose I just can't believe it's all over,' she added, with a wistful sadness her companion found oddly disturbing.

And it *was* all over, she kept telling herself on the drive that took her home. But her heart flatly refused to accept what it was being told, leaping in wild hope as the sleek white Mercedes drew up beside her the moment the police car sped away.

'Sally, I haven't much time . . . I'm on my way to the airport.'

'You'd best be on your way, then,' she retorted tonelessly, then turned and walked towards the house.

'What are you running from, Sally?' he demanded angrily, grasping her by the arm and spinning her round to face him as she reached the front door.

'Isn't it obvious?' she spat at him in fury, wrenching free her arm. 'And forgive me if I say no more—after all, you're the one who can't abide having the obvious pointed out to him!'

'You don't have to run away from me, Sally,' he told her wearily. 'Can't you see? I'd have tried to understand, if only you'd given me the chance . . .'

'Understand what?' she spat at him. 'My thieving tendencies?'

His jaw clenched angrily. 'Yes, even those. But it seems I'm wasting my time . . . I'll not compound that by also wasting my breath.'

He was close enough for her to be able to see the dark rings of tiredness beneath his eyes, and the anxious stab of love that pierced her was mingled with bitter resentment of the power he still so unknowingly wielded over her.

'Yes, you're wasting both your time and your breath,' she told him, the coldness in her voice her only victory against the love still raging in her heart. 'But surely it's worth it . . . you couldn't resist coming to gloat, could you, Paul?'

For a moment their eyes locked, blue blazing into blue. Then he sighed and half turned. 'No, I couldn't resist coming to gloat. Goodbye, Sally.'

She leaned against the cool dark wood of the door as she watched him retrace his steps down the drive.

All sensation, all awareness of her surroundings had left her. There was nothing, save the tall, athletic figure walking away from her—that turned as it reached the gate and, for several seconds, faced her before disappearing with a last, mocking salute. She heard the engine of the Mercedes throb to life, followed by the sound of tyres against the gravelled roadside. Then all she heard was the empty silence—the stark void that told her he had left her life for ever.

CHAPTER TEN

'EDDIE'S off with some of his conservation buddies for the day,' announced Lena Kapotwe, glancing up from a document she had been perusing, as Sally seated herself at the breakfast table. 'So you can't use him as an excuse for our not having a chat.'

Sally sighed as she helped herself to coffee and toast. 'I haven't really been using him as an excuse,' she protested lamely. 'You've only been back a couple of days... and just seeing the expression on his face makes other matters seem trivial.'

'I know.' For a moment Lena's eyes grew misty. 'It's as though he's been away for ten years and can't believe he's back... but that doesn't alter the fact that you and I still have things to discuss,' she added firmly. 'Sally, do you remember my saying there was a time I was loath to mention Mark's name for fear of upsetting you?'

'You can mention him all you wish,' replied Sally stiffly, deliberately misconstruing her friend's words as a familiar coldness clutched at her heart.

'Mark—yes,' responded Lena softly. 'But it's Paul Morrant's name that's creating the problem this time and, whether you like it or not, Sally, I'm not making the same mistake twice. He contacted me in England a couple of weeks ago, right after he got back from here...'

'Would you like some more coffee?' interrupted Sally coldly.

'No!' exclaimed the Zambian girl impatiently. 'What I'd like is for you to listen! You seem so wrapped up in your own private unhappiness that you appear to have

160

forgotten that the conservation programme could still be at stake,' she protested. 'Wincombe's trial starts any day now—or hadn't it even occurred to you there would be one?'

'Lena, I...' Sally broke off, shame staining her cheeks a hot red. 'I'm sorry...you're absolutely right, I've been...'

'You've been alone and unhappy, love,' murmured Lena gently. 'It doesn't take a genius to see that. But you're not alone any more, and using harsh words was the only way I could make you see that...and try to get you to listen to me.'

'I'm listening.' Sally threw her a wan, shame-faced smile.

'Sally, I don't know what went on between the two of you, but one thing I do know—Paul Morrant is bending over backwards to ensure there's no possible risk of backlash on the conservation programme. Not only is he making sure we aren't implicated, his bank is donating Zambezi Safaris' shortfall for this year.'

'How big-hearted of him,' exploded Sally bitterly. 'Considering how quick he was to drag us into it all in the first place!'

'It was Mark who got us into this,' pointed out Lena tartly. 'And, with the circumstantial evidence Interpol had, Morrant would have been a fool not to be suspicious. You're a rotten liar, love, and thanks to me you *were* lying to him...which would have made a man of his intelligence even more suspicious.'

'The truth wouldn't have made any difference to him,' exclaimed Sally harshly. 'You were right to make me keep it from him...he's totally inflexible.'

'If it's any consolation, Sally, he sounded every bit as bitter as you do,' murmured Lena, her face troubled.

'Why should *he* feel bitter?' demanded Sally furiously. 'Nobody had *him* arrested! Nobody had *him* thrown into prison like a common thief!'

With a troubled sigh, Lena hastily poured more coffee and slid a cup towards her glowering friend.

'Drink this,' she told her firmly. 'And stop making ridiculous statements. Nothing Paul Morrant could have said or done would have stopped your arrest. Had I been there, they'd have arrested me, too—so stop taking it all so personally. The circumstantial evidence was, unfortunately, very strong.'

'It didn't take them long to discover I was innocent,' argued Sally stubbornly.

'Long enough for you to have skipped the country had you been guilty, though,' pointed out Lena with infuriating logic. 'Anyway, that's neither here nor there now,' she sighed, fingering the document she had been examining when Sally arrived. 'I'd a pretty good idea what this was—so I took the liberty of opening it. You've been subpoenaed to give evidence at Wincombe's trial.'

Her face blank with disbelief, Sally took the document and read it, shaking her head from side to side as she did so.

'Mark rang earlier,' stated Lena. 'He's received one. We can also thank our lucky stars all charges of complicity have been dropped against him—and I feel sure we have Paul Morrant to thank for that. After all, Mark was still in our employ when Wincombe embarked on his thieving spree…and part of the proceeds were staking Mark's company.'

'No one in his right mind would have thought Mark involved in fraud,' snorted Sally. 'He's too stupid!'

'But stupidity is no plea under the law,' chuckled Lena. 'And there's a pretty fair chance a complicity charge would have held, had Morrant-Gervaise-Morrant pressed for it.'

Sally shrugged, then gave an unexpectedly warm smile. 'In a way, this enforced trip to London couldn't have come at a more opportune time.' The smile became a teasing grin under Lena's puzzled gaze. 'I was planning to disappear for a while, anyway—to give you two love-birds a bit of time on your own,' she teased. Though London, she reminded herself grimly, was the last place on earth she would have chosen.

'And there's no reason why he should be in court,' blurted out Lena uneasily.

'He?' admonished Sally gently. 'I thought you were dispensing with the rigmarole of avoiding certain names. Lena, I know I seem to have a pretty disastrous record with the men in my life—but I think we can safely put this one down to a bad dose of infatuation.'

Lena treated her to a look that tried desperately to mask its scepticism, then gave a small shrug. Her face brightened a little as she tapped the bulky envelope beside her.

'They've provided first-class tickets . . . not to mention arrangements for the swish hotel you'll be staying in,' she declared brightly.

The flight, first class though it was, had one decided drawback—it was the one on which Mark Shelby had also been booked. On it, Sally had managed to avoid him simply by sitting as far away from him as possible and pretending to sleep for almost the entire journey.

Her luck ran out at Heathrow airport when she dashed to get a taxi and found him hot on her heels.

'Darling, don't you think you're being a bit childish? After all, we . . .'

'Mark, do me a favour, will you?' She rounded on him angrily. 'And stop calling me darling.'

'OK, OK. But at least we can share a taxi.' Sally groaned inwardly as he gave the driver the name of his hotel—the one into which she had also been booked.

'Sally, I know I was the one to land you and Zambezi Safaris in all this, but it wasn't deliberate, and you can hardly go on punishing me for ever because of it,' he complained, giving her what she supposed was meant to be an irresistible smile.

'You, Mark, are totally irresponsible,' she told him curtly. 'And the less I have to do with you, the better I'll like it.'

'I thought you'd got the lectures off your chest the last time we met,' he complained, his expression truculent. 'For God's sake, how many times do I have to say I'm sorry?'

'Since the last time we met,' she informed him, her voice shaking with fury, 'you skipped away from police surveillance and I spent a night in the cells—a delight I could have avoided had you been around to explain all the money that had been incorrectly credited to our trading account.

'Your opinion of me certainly couldn't be lower, could it, Sally?' he demanded angrily.

Having no intention of being drawn into a verbal spate with him, Sally turned her face towards the window. She was tired and feeling devastatingly depressed, and already the cold dampness of the bleak November morning seemed to be seeping through to her bones. All she wanted was to get to the hotel, have a warming bath and collapse into her bed.

'Josh rang me when he and Wincombe arrived at the hospital in Chipata.'

Sally peered doggedly through the window, determined to blot out the insistent drone of Mark's voice.

'When you and Morrant hadn't turned up the next day, I had no option but to go looking for you—I was half out of my mind with worry.'

Sally swung round to face him, guilt, confusion and exasperation battling on her face.

'Mark, do you never stop to examine the possible consequences of what you're doing?' she groaned. 'Look—I'm sorry, I should at least have given you the benefit of the doubt...but I've had this wretched business up to the eyeballs. And having to come here to give evidence is just the last straw.'

'Don't worry, dar...Sally,' he corrected himself quickly. 'You're forgiven.'

Sally's eyes flew back to the window as her mouth clamped firmly shut. If she started telling him, as forcefully as she felt inclined, that no apology had been intended, she would probably end up screaming at him, given her present frame of mind.

The bath had eased the chill from her, but it had done nothing to alleviate the tiredness and depression that left her feeling so peculiarly detached and drained.

She was just about to climb into bed when a rap on the door brought an exclamation of weary protest to her lips.

'Coffee and croissants—you looked as though you could do with them.' Mark strode through the door Sally had just opened and, with a flourish, deposited a tray on the bedside table.

'Mark, what I need is a couple of hours of uninterrupted sleep,' she protested wearily, noting, with a stab of irritation, that the tray was laid out for two.

'Heaven knows why you need more sleep—that's all you did for the entire journey.' Seating himself on the bed, Mark proceeded to fill two cups. 'I particularly noticed that you had no breakfast, so be a good girl and eat and drink up.'

Rather than waste time arguing, Sally reluctantly decided to comply. Now was as good a time as any to make it clear that cosy get-togethers here, or anywhere else, would never again feature in their relationship.

'Mark, there are a few things you and I need to get straight...' Another rap on the door cut her off, bringing a groan of impatience from her as she returned to open it.

'Sally, I...' Paul Morrant's words broke off as he glanced over her shoulder to where Mark sat on her bed sipping coffee. 'I needn't have troubled myself; it appears you've settled in very comfortably.' His voice was as cold as the eyes that raked down her dressing-gowned body before he bowed with a chilling formality.

Then he turned and left, before Sally had had a chance to utter a single word.

'So...that, I take it, was the dashing international banker in person,' murmured Mark, his eyes narrowing in speculation as they rested on Sally's ashen features.

'What makes you assume that?' asked Sally stiffly— her stomach felt as though it had been used as a punch-bag.

'Let's just say I appear to have discovered a sixth sense I never realised I possessed,' he replied thoughtfully.

'If any such sense exists, which I very much doubt, it would have warned you against waltzing in here expecting a cosy breakfast for two,' retorted Sally angrily.

'My poor Sally,' he murmured, the expression of speculation still on his face as he rose to his feet. 'Despite your brains and beauty, you don't have much luck with the men in your life, do you?'

'Just go, will you, Mark?' she asked tonelessly. 'I'm tired and I want to get some sleep.'

He turned to face her when he reached the door. 'I'd be the first to admit I was bad news as far as you were concerned—though, given the chance, we could have worked it out. But a man like Morrant is way out of your league, I promise you.'

'I've no idea what you're talking about,' she retorted icily. 'Except that the *pair* of you are bad news as far as I'm concerned. You, because you got me into this mess in the first place, and he, because he had me branded as a virtual criminal. So it should come as no surprise to either of you to learn that you're the last two people I would wish to have anything to do with for a very long time to come.'

The last thing she glimpsed on his face, before he closed the door behind him, was the same look of scepticism that she had seen on Lena's face.

Tears of pure frustration were streaming down her face as she finally climbed into bed. In Lusaka, she had almost succeeded in convincing herself she was beginning to cope—that the pain of the immediate past, though still there, was under control.

All it had taken was the sound of his voice—the crushing impact of his physical presence—and she was trapped once more in the agony of an endless nightmare.

At least he had not come here, Sally told herself as for the fourth day she made her way up the wide stone steps to the court. But there was little comfort in that thought. For three days she had sat as voices droned relentlessly around her.

She had tried to drum up an element of pity for the slight figure of Jonathan Wincombe as he took the stand, but had been unable to shake off the old conviction that the man was somehow enjoying his brief moment of notoriety.

She had tried to listen and to understand all that was being said, but had found it impossible as, time and again, her mind had become filled with images of nothing and no one but Paul Morrant. She now faced this fourth day with no more than a weary resignation. Whatever might occur, it would lack the power to drag her mind from its own, inevitable, train of thought.

'We're quite likely to be called on to give evidence today.'

Sally turned and found Mark beside her.

Since that morning of their arrival, there had been an atmosphere of almost strained formality between them. Though neither had deliberately gone out of the way to avoid the other, they had met infrequently and then had exchanged only a few polite words.

'I suppose getting up on the witness stand will provide a little relief from this interminable boredom,' added Mark, now treating her to a smile that might once have tugged at her heartstrings, she realised with a mild sense of incredulity.

'I can think of several more appealing ways of relieving boredom,' she replied with a wry smile, her eyes gazing past him to alight idly on the large, chauffeur-driven car drawing up at the kerb below.

Her idleness was gone the instant the tall, familiar figure stepped out of the car, broad shoulders hunching themselves against the cold as he drew up the collar of his coat. When he turned, it was almost as though he had heard his name called, and he looked directly up into her mesmerised eyes. His hands remained where they were, immobile against the dark navy of his lapels, while time ground slowly to a breathless halt. Sally was conscious of seeing eyes then an entire face, so utterly devoid of all expression it was as though her gaze had been transfixed by that of a marble statue.

'Sally?' Mark's voice penetrated an invisible barrier, restoring the dimension of time.

She turned to him with an imperceptible shiver. 'Let's go in, Mark. It's freezing out here.'

Scarcely conscious of what she was doing, she slipped her hand through Mark's arm, turning her back on the still figure of the only man to whom she had ever truly given her love.

Even while Mark gave his evidence, Sally found it impossible to prevent her eyes from straying to that navy-clad figure a few rows ahead of her—to the memory-invoking thickness of hair that curled lazily against the dark collar as he now and then tilted back his head.

She tried desperately to concentrate on what Mark was saying, reminding herself that all it would take was a careless slip of his tongue—a mere mention of the name Zambezi Safaris—and all could be lost. Her ears kept their separate vigil for those two fatal words, while her mind remained lost in the distraction of Paul Morrant's inescapable presence.

When Mark stood down from the box and a lunch recess was declared, Sally heaved a huge sigh of relief as an insupportable burden seemed to lift from her shoulders.

'No, I honestly don't feel like eating,' she stated in reply to Mark's suggestion as they stepped out into the corridor.

'Miss Hughes?'

She turned and nodded at the tall, grey-haired man who had approached her.

'Would you mind coming with me?'

Again she nodded, assuming it to have something to do with the evidence she was to give. With an apologetic shrug in Mark's direction, she followed.

'I'll see you back in court,' she called to him as she left. She was ushered into a high-ceilinged room, its gloomy vastness relieved only by a heavy wood desk and a few leather-bound chairs. As the door closed behind her she sensed movement by one of the tall, velvet-draped windows to the right of her.

'Why have I been brought here?' she demanded stiffly, as Paul Morrant turned from the window to face her.

The heavy, immaculately cut coat was unbuttoned, revealing the dark elegance of the suit beneath and, for a moment, Sally's heart brought her a memory of that same lithe body, clad only in jeans and with the sheen of heat on its sun-kissed skin.

'You will be called on to give evidence this afternoon.' The cold impersonality of his tone ripped through her memories, rendering them no more than fragments of a disappearing dream.

'I've no idea what I could possibly say that hasn't been said already.' Her tone was colourless.

'For a start, it would be politic for you not to mention Zambezi Safaris by name, no matter what.'

'If I'm asked, I can hardly refuse to answer,' she retorted, unnerved by his tone.

'If asked,' he intoned, with exaggerated patience, 'you describe the general nature of the company—you do not name it.'

'I'm surprised I'm being asked to testify at all, considering how incompetent you obviously find me. Why don't you instruct your QC...'

'He's not my QC.' The drawled words cut through hers. 'This case happens to be the Crown versus

Wincombe, or hadn't you noticed? And as you seemed quite prepared to sell your soul to the devil for the sake of your precious company in the past, I was under the impression you'd be glad of any advice that was going now.'

'And you call stating the obvious advice, do you?' she demanded angrily.

'How strange that you should recognise it as such,' he murmured with icy contempt, 'when the obvious seems to be something you're normally quite blind to.'

'Do you get some sort of kick out of humiliating people?' Her words were wooden as she fought back tears. 'If so, you can have your kicks now—you deserve them! You see, I *am* indebted to you for the protection you've given Zambezi Safaris ... as you so rightly said, I'd sell my soul, even to a devil like you, to keep the company going.'

'And your body, Sally?' he asked with chilling venom. 'Is that still part of the deal? Or does Shelby have a say in the matter now? The man you once thought you loved ... before me, that is.'

The force with which Sally hit his face was such that she felt the swelling begin in her palm even in the instant before her wrist was clamped in the vice of his fingers.

'Have I touched a raw nerve, my darling?' His words dripped like ice on her ears. 'Don't you like to be reminded of your love for me?'

'Let go of me,' she pleaded brokenly, her eyes locked on the reddening imprint of her hand on his cheek, because they could not bear to witness the contempt in the glittering coldness of his eyes.

'Who do you love now, Sally?' he whispered softly, slowly drawing her towards him.

'I hate you.' Her words were a husky protest. 'It's Mark I love!' she lied in panic, as he trapped her head in his hands, forcing it still while his mouth sought hers. 'I love Mark,' she protested brokenly in that moment before her lips opened in treacherous welcome to his.

It did not matter that the harsh demand of his mouth inflicted a searing, bruising pain on her lips. All that mattered was his touch, the physical nearness of him and, for a moment that was no more than a madness, she was melting in response to that longed-for familiarity of him. Then came the faint echo of sanity forcing its way through that terrible madness and she was fighting to be free.

'So, you love Mark, do you?' he rasped hoarsely, his arms dropping to his sides.

'I love Mark,' she echoed in a scarcely audible whisper, and turned from him.

He made no move to stop her as she walked to the door.

'You should try convincing your body of that, Sally. It seems strangely unaware of the fact.'

She turned and looked at him. He had returned to the window, his back towards her.

'What were you trying to prove, Paul?' she asked, unable to prevent pain from spilling into her words.

'Nothing,' he replied with a harsh laugh of bitterness. 'It was just a case of the male ego rearing its ugly head.' Suddenly he spun round to face her. 'Sally, why is it that with you I find myself saying things I neither mean nor want to say?' he demanded.

'Perhaps with me, the truth just slips out,' she retorted bitterly.

'You once observed that you seemed to bring out the worst in me,' he muttered hoarsely, as though lost in private thought. 'You do. But there was also a time I felt you brought out the best in me.'

'You don't have to remind me,' she rasped angrily, her fingers clenching tightly around the huge brass doorknob. 'I believe that was the very time you were plotting to have me thrown into jail. If that's the best of you, Paul, I find the worst preferable—infinitely preferable!'

With a heart that felt as though it were splintering into a thousand pieces, she began opening the door.

'Sally...for God's sake, what's wrong with us? We seem incapable of talking to one another.'

Something in his tone rooted her to the spot.

'Before I left Lusaka, there were things I should have said to you—things I wanted to say...but I got nowhere. I went to your hotel the morning you arrived...again to try to say those things.' He gave a shrug of resignation. 'This, my third attempt, has got me no further than the other two.'

'I always suspected you had a pretty low opinion of my powers of reasoning—but even I'm not stupid enough to require any explanation from you,' she hurled at him angrily, silently branding herself a fool for even thinking she had heard an alien pleading in his tone. It had been entirely in her imagination.

'Are you telling me there isn't a single doubt in your mind, Sally?' he asked, with a gentleness that had nothing to do with her imagination.

Her eyes, dark with confusion and anguish, met his as she strove to utter the words of dismissal that refused to come.

'All I ask is that we meet after today's proceedings—and that you hear what I have to say. Will you agree to that, Sally?'

She wanted to cry out her rejection of what he asked, but there were still no words. Instead she nodded wearily, then slipped quickly through the door.

Her mind was in a complete daze as she retraced her steps and found Mark, and it remained in a state of numb detachment when she later took the stand and answered the handful of what seemed to her to be inconsequential questions.

It was only later, when she was seated once more beside Mark in the courtroom, that awareness began penetrating the barrier of numbness.

'I don't know about you, Sally, but I've had my fill of hanging around here—how about playing truant for once?' whispered Mark conspiratorially.

For a moment, Sally was sorely tempted. Paul had not returned to the courtroom for the afternoon's proceedings, but she had little doubt he would be waiting for her when they ended.

She gave a small smile as she shook her head at Mark, instantly regretting her decision when he rose and, with a farewell grin in her direction, left.

She should have gone with Mark, she chided herself frustratedly, instead of hanging round for the inevitable humiliation that would come with Paul's words of explanation.

He was hardly the first man to have succumbed to physical desire despite strong mental reservations. Though few such men, she felt certain, would be thick-skinned enough to insist on spelling out the whys and wherefores to the woman concerned.

There was a grim set to her mouth as she later descended the steps of the building and saw the white BMW waiting at the kerb. She hesitated as she saw Paul Morrant at the wheel, watching as he spotted her and broke off his exchange with a woman traffic warden with her pad at the ready, and impatiently waved her to hurry. 'Sorry to rush you,' he apologised, blowing a departing kiss in the direction of the traffic warden and speeding away. 'Seems I was on a double yellow line—not that there's anything but those within a mile of here.'

His tone was surprisingly relaxed—chatty, almost— but Sally remained silent, devoting her entire attention to doing up her seat-belt.

With her seat-belt checked and double-checked, she gazed sightlessly down at her hands, now tightly clasped on her lap, wondering what on earth could have poss- essed her to place herself in such a self-destructive situation.

'Where are we going?' she demanded suddenly, de- ciding she could stand the self-imposed silence no longer.

'I've a place in Chelsea—I thought it wiser for us to go there, rather than risk one of our voluble talks in public.'

'It won't be one of *our* voluble talks,' she retorted coldly. 'You'll be doing all the talking—I have nothing to say.'

'I still consider my place safer,' he replied, an edge erasing the previous relaxation from his tone.

Sally glanced across at him—then, for her own peace of mind, trained her eyes on the traffic ahead.

Just the sight of him sent a host of conflicting emotions racing through her—just the sight of those strong, tanned hands lightly gripping the steering wheel was enough to dredge up memories she would have gladly buried beneath a ton of concrete.

CHAPTER ELEVEN

By the time they drew up outside a row of white-fronted mews cottages in a cobbled street, Sally was feeling less at ease and more resentful than she could ever remember feeling before. Much of her resentment was directed towards herself.

Only an out and out masochist would have let herself in for what she was about to go through, she raged silently as she followed the tall, aloof figure of her silent companion through a highly polished mahogany front door.

He might have started out sounding chatty, but he had certainly reverted to type quickly enough, she fumed, stepping into the hall and on to the dark gleam of parquet. He had not even taken the trouble to ask how she had fared on the witness stand. Her thoughts were angry, random—they were all she had to distract her from the dreadful prospect of what lay ahead. But even those protective thoughts were momentarily swept from her mind by the blast of heat that suddenly enveloped her.

Almost reeling from its intensity, she began automatically unbuttoning her coat.

With a softly muttered oath, Paul reached out and took the coat from her, then removed both his and the suit jacket beneath.

'I apologise for this sweltering atmosphere,' he offered, his tone oddly tentative. 'I dropped in earlier to turn up the heating... I wasn't sure if you were acclimatised to London yet.'

Sally looked at him uncertainly, her anger treacherously deserting her at the sight of his small shrug of embarrassment.

'I didn't realise it would be this overpoweringly effective,' he added, sounding decidedly ill at ease.

'Perhaps you should turn it down a little,' she suggested, troubled to hear the same hesitancy reflected in her own voice.

He nodded. 'Would you like tea? Coffee, perhaps?'

'No, thank you.' They were like a pair of strangers, she suddenly realised: polite, guarded—each treading warily with the other.

'If you'd like to go through there,' he suggested, indicating a door to the left of her. 'I'll join you in a moment.' For a split second, their eyes met—uncertain, half-questioning—till Sally nodded, breaking the contact, and moved towards the door.

It was almost as though he were dreading this every bit as much as she was, she thought, nonplussed, then immediately began dismissing such a ridiculous idea as she entered a large, starkly elegant and beautifully furnished room. A room that reflected the taste of a wealthy, self-assured and undeniably cultured man, she reminded herself sharply—but a man who knew no doubts and who was certainly a stranger to the dread that now filled her. He was manipulating her, just as he always had, she warned herself, as she sat down on a large armchair, part of a matching suite in fine yellow velvet so pale it was almost the colour of rich cream.

He had always manipulated her, repeated a small warning voice as her eyes began to stray, becoming captivated by what they beheld. It was such a beautiful room, she thought wistfully as she gazed down at the soft muted pastels of the Indian rug at her feet. Her glance moved along the room, past a huge, marbled fireplace, resting for a moment on the dark surround of a highly polished wood where the large palely contrasting rug ended. Then her gaze rose to a small, intricately carved walnut table in a far corner of the room, where a flowering succulent spilled its crimson petals in untidy profusion on the gleaming surface.

She dragged her bewitched eyes away, forcing them to concentrate as she rolled the sleeves of her warm wool dress to the elbows. She frowned as the dark green of the material clung in restricting tightness against the golden tan of her arms and quickly rolled each sleeve down a turn—she would break out in a heat rash any moment now, she told herself fretfully. She pulled herself up sharply, unsettled by her constantly yo-yoing thoughts.

'It should ease off fairly soon. I've turned it right down.' Sally started at those quiet words and glanced up. He stood at the doorway and had, she noted with a stab of envy, removed his tie and undone the top few buttons of his shirt.

'Do you feel very uncomfortable?' he asked, the hesitancy still marked in his tone as he entered the room.

'No...I...' She gave a groan of exasperation. 'Of course I feel uncomfortable!' she blurted out, as he halted by the fireplace. 'Paul...what possible point can there be to this?' she begged, her words petering to a hoarse whisper as hopelessness gained the upper hand over the panic welling up inside her.

'Perhaps none. But we'll never know if we don't have it out.' He was standing at right angle to the fireplace, facing her. As he spoke, she saw the sudden clenching of his hands as he rammed them into his trouser pockets before tilting his body sideways till one shoulder rested against the mantelshelf.

There was unmistakable tension in every line of that tall, lean-hipped body—tension in the slight hunching of the broad, sloping shoulders and, most of all, in the tightly clenched set of the jaw.

'For once I'd like us to talk to one another... with no shouting, no fighting,' he muttered, the complete remoteness on his handsome face accentuating the hollow chill in his tone. 'Just to talk, and have the truth...to hear the reason for your lies.'

The anger that flared in her died in the instant his eyes met hers—stilled by a bleakness that was frozen in pain. 'Why?' she croaked in dazed disbelief. 'When you know... when I've already admitted I lied? What more do you want?' she demanded, her voice hardening.

'Forget what you assume I know...'

'I assume?' she cut in bitterly.

'Just tell me...all that you hid from me. Please, Sally.'

She froze as the harshness deserted his voice, leaving his final words ringing in her ears like an agonised plea. Her eyes flew questioningly to his tense, waiting figure, then her shoulders sagged in defeat. It was futile to try to understand him... all she could do was accept that she had given her love, in its entirety, to a man whose mind she could never even begin to understand.

Like an automaton, she began to speak. And even as she spoke those words it had been her instinct to tell him from the start, there was a ghostly voice of awareness in her—telling her she had been tricked into participating in a charade that could only bring her humiliation—but that voice lacked the strength of the eyes that held hers and had no power to silence the words that tumbled tonelessly from her lips.

Long before she had finished, she was aware of a restlessness in him. At first he took a hand from his pocket and dragged impatient fingers through the black thickness of his hair. Then that same hand rubbed distractedly at the back of his neck, before dropping back to the pocket from which it had been removed, the thumb hooking into the vent while the fingers began an erratic drumming against the dark navy cloth.

'And you thought I'd withdraw my support for the conservation programme had I found out?' he asked coldly, as she finished.

'No...I...Lena was convinced you would—that's why she made me promise not to tell you.'

'I asked what *you* had thought, Sally,' he pointed out quietly.

She gave a small shrug. 'I actually tried to tell you once...in Luangwa...but you'd fallen asleep.' Her eyes met his defiantly. 'Which was just as well, considering my promise to Lena.'

'But you would have told me, if not for that?'

She nodded, anger darkening her eyes. 'And if I'd had any inkling of your true suspicions,' she informed him coldly, 'I'd obviously have told you.'

'Ah—the money,' he murmured, his tone brittle. 'Did it never occur to you that all you had to do was ask? In fact, you didn't even have to stoop that low, did you, Sally? I underwrote what Zambezi Safaris needed for the conservation team without you having to say a word.' The mocking travesty of a smile that accompanied his words only increased her bewildered confusion.

She shifted uncomfortably in her seat. 'Paul, I am grateful for what you've done...but I don't understand why you should sound so accusing...'

'Don't you really, Sally?' he asked quietly, moving to her side with deceptive speed as his tone brought her angrily to her feet. 'How else would you expect me to sound, when there are still lies unexplained?' he murmured chillingly. He dropped to his haunches as she sank down again.

'Paul, I want to leave,' she stated tonelessly.

'No deal, Sally,' he told her with soft finality. 'You haven't yet explained why you want me to believe you don't love me.'

Even as she recoiled from it, the mesmerising caress in his words sent a shiver rippling through her.

'Nor how you could possibly expect me to believe that anything, short of love, made me the first...the only man to have shared the magic of your passion.'

'Stop it!' she begged hoarsely, shaking her head from side to side to disperse those softly taunting words.

'What sort of fool do you take me for?' he demanded harshly. 'Telling me you loved Shelby, while everything in you cried out your love for me.'

'How about pride, Paul?' she retorted, her voice cold with shock. 'That vital commodity you're so determined to strip from me.' She clenched her hands tightly in her lap to halt their uncontrolled shaking. 'You see, that's all it was that made me say I loved Mark,' she continued bitterly. 'The last shreds of a pride that couldn't face your knowing I love you...knowing you would never love me in return.'

'No,' he whispered hoarsely, leaping to his feet and gazing down at her, the intensity of his expression heightened by a ghostly pallor. 'I had convinced myself it was shame,' he intoned distractedly, pacing back and forth. 'Every bit of evidence they dug up pointed to your involvement...in the end I couldn't take any more.' He spun to face her mid-stride, his eyes dark with the reflection of an inner conflict. 'I thought it was shame for what you'd done...forcing you to reject me...Sally, have you any idea what I'm saying?' he groaned raggedly. 'I'm the biggest fool around!' he protested, the strange intensity in his eyes disturbing her even more than the burning imprint of the hand that drew her gently towards him.

'Let go of me,' she implored, the uncertain words forced through lips so numb they scarcely moved.

'Oh, no,' he murmured softly, his fingers slipping down to clasp her lifeless hand. 'Not till you understand the full extent of my insanity. You see, almost from the moment we met, a black cloud has hovered over my life—the devastating knowledge that all evidence pointed to the woman I couldn't stop myself loving being part of Wincombe's fraud. And by the time my heart was insisting you couldn't have been involved, it was all too late—the wheels had been set in motion and none of my efforts could halt them.'

'The woman you what?' she croaked inanely, as her world ran completely out of control, then crashed to a resounding halt.

'The woman I would have still loved had I discovered she was running every illegal racket the length and breadth of Africa.'

She reached out blindly, feeling her second hand taken in the warmth of his as she willed the unresponsive void of her mind to clear.

'Sally, I love you,' he whispered huskily, his hands guiding her numbed body till he was drawing her down on the sofa beside him. 'I love you,' he repeated softly, cocooning her in the familiar strength of his arms, where the heavy beat of his heart throbbed its insistent message through the fog of her mind. 'Oh, Sally, try to forgive me,' he pleaded brokenly. 'Put your arms around me and tell me you can forgive me.'

His lips nuzzled against her cheek, then were searching in desperate hunger against those that turned in tremulous uncertainty to his.

'This isn't happening!' she cried out in sobbing protest, her lips denying his even as her arms moved hesitantly, then clung in fierce desperation to him.

'It's happening, my darling,' he promised huskily, his arms crushing her to him, willing her to believe. 'Don't cry, please, Sally, I can't bear it if you cry,' he begged, rocking her gently against him.

'I'm not crying,' she protested incoherently, then began pushing him from her with all the strength she could muster, to glare at him through tear-dimmed eyes. 'It doesn't matter what you do—what you say—I don't believe any of this is happening...'

'Of course you don't,' he soothed gently. 'How could you possibly be anything other than completely confused with an idiot like me loving you? But it's a very real love, my sweet Sally. Tell me how I can convince you,' he urged, his voice and his face filled with a gentle tenderness that started up cracks in the dam of disbelief within her.

'Your eyes were so cold,' she protested, gazing into eyes that were now softly languorous as he took her arms and placed them round his neck.

'They lied...but not always, did they, Sally?' he coaxed softly.

'No...not always,' she murmured in a far-away voice, half remembering, and half conscious of the dam within her threatening to crumble with the promise of the existence of a happiness so powerful it would explode into every part of her being, if only she would let it.

She felt his lips move against her cheek, the gentle balm of their random, butterfly kisses filling her with a breathless, hopeful expectancy.

'Sally, there's so much love for you in me...tell me I wasn't always successful in hiding it from you,' he begged. 'Hell, I was practically a text-book schizophrenic . . . half of me plotting to put you away for life for what I thought you'd done . . . the other half plotting to spring you from jail should it ever happen!'

Her reaction to the bewildered indignation in his voice was instant and instinctive. The hands that caressed his head, the lips that rained gentle, comforting kisses on his troubled face, did so in blind response to an overwhelming surge of love.

'For God's sake, what am I doing?' she groaned protestingly, suddenly complete aware of her actions. 'How can I possibly love a man as stupid as you?' she objected, her lips now answering the snatched, impassioned kisses instigated by his. 'How could you? Paul, how could you?' she choked in outrage, her hands trembling as they compulsively traced the outline of his beloved face—still not entirely convinced their touch could be anything other than a dream. 'To think I love a fool,' she whispered, the dam within her shattering as the force of happiness spilled free. 'A complete and utter fool,' she marvelled, her words a breathless mixture of love, laughter and incredulous delight.

'Call me all the names you like,' he murmured contentedly. 'I deserve them all . . . your love is the only thing that matters.'

It was the love gleaming in the heavy-lidded darkness of his eyes that brought a choking sensation of joy to her as he gazed down at her, his arms tightening compulsively around her.

'Have I really—completely and without a shred of doubt—convinced you that I love you?'

She nodded. There were words she wanted to say, but her vocal cords refused to co-operate.

'I don't deserve to be let off so lightly,' he murmured huskily, his nose rubbing gently against hers. 'I don't deserve you . . . oh, Sally, when I think of how my mindless stupidity turned both our lives into a ghastly nightmare...how could I ever hope for your forgiveness?'

'Perhaps I should rant like a fishwife for an hour or so,' she teased, her heart so full of happiness that pain was a rapidly fading memory.

'Not that,' he groaned, his laughter a husky throb of delight. 'Not even I could deserve something as hellish as that.'

'What you deserve is the most evil, the most pro-longed punishment anyone could ever devise,' she told him softly, her fingers luxuriating in the tousled thickness of his hair as he buried his face against her. With a soft chuckle she yanked him up by his hair.

'Unfortunately for me, but most fortunately for you, punishing you would be tantamount to punishing myself... only a thousand times less bearable.'

The smile that began as a tentative curve at the corners of his mouth grew till it was a dazzling, breath-stopping statement of love that sharpened the joy in her almost to the point of pain.

'My pain threshold's abnormally low where you're concerned.' He cupped her face in his hands as the smile died to sadness on his face. 'I'd give anything to be able to turn back the clock—to be able to say the words of love that cried out silently within me that first time we made love. Because it was never anything less than love that you and I made... just that I was too big a fool to allow myself to say the words.'

'My poor, foolish Paul,' she whispered huskily, her face bathed in love as she tried to coax the sadness from his.

'And your poor, foolish Paul was half out of his mind with his first, and utterly devastating, taste of jealousy... what the hell was Shelby doing in your room that morning you arrived?' he demanded suddenly, then buried his face against her cheek with a soft, disbelieving groan.

'You were actually jealous?' she murmured incredulously, her fingers caressing in his hair as she held him close.

'I wasn't sure who I should throttle first—you or him,' he muttered, disgruntled, his teeth a threatening sharpness as they nibbled against the corner of her mouth.

'I suppose he was trying to rekindle a flame that had never really existed,' she told him gently, then went on to tell him of her relationship with Mark, its ending, and what had passed between them since. 'It took loving you to show me I had never really loved him . . . losing Mark was like a mild headache. Whereas losing you . . .' Her voice caught on the chill bleakness of memory. 'Paul, it was like an unending death by torture.'

'You never lost me, my darling, and you never will,' he promised huskily, his hands moving in gentle comfort against her. 'How could I feel so insanely jealous when I knew you loved me?' he groaned in angry disbelief. 'How could a grown man, an allegedly intelligent man, have possibly behaved as I did? The most crucial period in my life . . . and I acted like a half-witted juvenile . . . like a mindless moron!'

'Would you mind not speaking about the man I love in such derogatory terms?' admonished Sally breathlessly, happiness scurrying through her with total abandon. 'Even if they are the truth.'

His laughter was a soft ripple of satisfaction—a caress of delight that sent her senses reeling as his arms tightened possessively around her.

'Love this man a lot, do you?' he teased, his body shifting lazily against hers, bringing heightened awareness to every nerve in her as his lips nuzzled sensuously at the hollow of her throat.

'With all my heart, and my body and my soul.' She shivered as his hands began moving in soft seduction against her body then gently began undoing the buttons of her dress.

'Is that the best you can offer?' he demanded huskily, his fingers trespassing beneath the material, leaving a trail of exquisite sensation on her flesh with the trembling delicacy of their touch.

'What more do you want?' she gasped, her senses swamped by the urgent quickening of the body straining ever closer to hers.

'Everything,' he whispered hoarsely, his breath a hot gasp as his mouth began exploring the corner of hers. 'I want every last scrap of you . . . and then some more.'

'OK, have the lot,' she murmured breathlessly, struggling to keep her mind intact as his hands and body grew more insistent. 'Just as long as you don't expect my sympathy.'

His laughter was a ragged, protesting groan. 'Sympathy?' he growled huskily. 'There won't be a day in your life when I'm not wreaking retribution for what you've put me through!'

'You brought it on yourself by being such an ostrich,' she gasped, her hands on his back alive to the taut ripple of muscles playing beneath them.

'Stop carping and tell me if we can get married here— or do we have to haul ourselves all the way back to Lusaka?' he whispered, becoming totally preoccupied as his tongue began tracing the outline of her lower lip with tantalising deliberation.

Sally was holding her breath as the world went into a dizzying spin and happiness exploded and consumed her.

'There's one small problem,' she managed, despite the severe problems she was having with her breathing.

'I should have known it,' he groaned, then gave a soft, throaty chuckle. 'Enlighten me.'

'Apart from all this retribution you plan wreaking— is it also in your plans that I should do the proposing?'

She gave a small shiver of excitement as another lazy chuckle rippled through him.

'Actually, I was planning on doing a deal with Aggie— I've a feeling she'd pay through the nose to get you off her hands.' He cupped her face in his hands, the laughter gone as he gazed down at her. 'Darling, you and I have a tendency to express our love in the strangest of ways. Sometimes in blazing rows, sometimes in laughter...I dare say we always shall, at times,' he told her softly.

As Sally nodded, she was aware of a happiness so complete that there was no part of her free from it.

'But not always,' he whispered. 'Do you remember a time when you woke up and reached out your arms to me, telling me you loved me?'

Again she nodded, her arms holding him now as they had then.

'There are times when even you and I will need plain words—and your words of love were the most beautiful sound I've ever heard, and they couldn't have come any plainer. I want you to marry me, and I want you to know that you and happiness are one to me. And, most of all, I want you to know that I shall spend the rest of my life cherishing and nurturing that happiness...if you'll only let me. Will you, my darling?'

'Yes, oh yes,' she whispered, her face bathed in the brilliance of love.

'When?' he demanded, his lips returning to nuzzle and search against her.

'The soonest moment we possibly can,' she begged, her lips following the example of his.

'That soon? Seems as though I'm the one who'll be obliged to display a few principles in this partnership,' he murmured, his lazy breathless chuckle playing even further havoc with her senses. 'We'll have to do the decent thing and round up at least Aggie and Alphonse. Then, of course, there's my mother...and Lena and her husband...hell, it's going to take for ever!'

His lips left a trail of suffocating excitement in their wake as they moved to the curve of her throat, and it occurred to Sally that there had been something of vital importance she had been about to say...but his arms had tightened fiercely around her. She bent her lips to the tousled blackness of his hair and her ears were filled with the soft caress of his words of love.

And she knew that, whatever it was she had meant to say, it could wait...the rest of her life would be cocooned in the strength of the love of this exciting, unpredictable man who had become her everything...there would be all the time in the world for the words she wished to tell him.

"Barbara Delinsky has a butterfly's touch for
nuance that brings an exquisite sheen to her
work."
—*Romantic Times*

A nightmare begins for a young woman when she
testifies in an arson trial. Fearing for her life, she
assumes a new identity... only to risk it all for love and
passion after meeting a handsome lawyer.

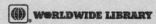

Harlequin American Romance

Romances that go one step farther...
American Romance

Realistic stories involving people you can relate to and
care about.

Compelling relationships between the mature men and
women of today's world.

Romances that capture the core of genuine emotions
between a man and a woman.

Join us each month for four new titles wherever paperback
books are sold.
Enter the world of American Romance.

Amro-1

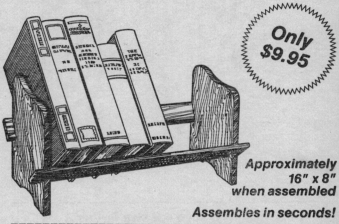